"Are you trying to convince me of something?" he asked roughly.

"No. I've just told you how I feel."

"Maybe I should show you what *I'm* feeling." He gave her a few moments to run. She knew he expected her to run.

But she held steadfast. "What *are* you feeling, Clay?"

His arms circled her, his lips came down on hers, and her breath became trapped in her chest along with the knowledge that he was trying to prove a point. She was unclear about that point, though, as his lips sealed to hers. And as she kissed him back, bringing her hands to his shoulders, gripping him tightly so her knees wouldn't buckle.

Dear Reader,

At my high school reunion, I reconnected with women I'd once confided in as we attended classes and dances and shared dreams. Guys who'd once seemed unapproachable were now easy to converse with. Time and experience seemed to have given most of us a kinder perspective. That reunion gave me the idea for my Reunion Brides miniseries.

High school classmates Celeste, Jenny and Mikala have stayed in touch. In *His Daughter…Their Child,* Celeste's friends watch as a spark ignites between her and Clay Sullivan at the reunion. Once a surrogate for Clay and her twin sister, Celeste is now determined to become a mother to the child her sister abandoned. Will attraction between Clay and Celeste ruin that possibility or give it wings?

Of course, I will be writing romances for Jenny and Mikala, too. Readers can follow my progress on my fan page at Facebook and visit my website at www.karenrosesmith.com for updates and excerpts.

Have a wonderful, romance-filled year.

All my best,

Karen Rose Smith

HIS DAUGHTER... THEIR CHILD

KAREN ROSE SMITH

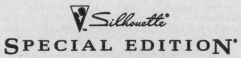

Published by Silhouette Books

America's Publisher of Contemporary Romance

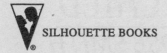 SILHOUETTE BOOKS

Recycling programs
for this product may
not exist in your area.

ISBN-13: 978-0-373-65580-9

HIS DAUGHTER...THEIR CHILD

Copyright © 2011 by Karen Rose Smith

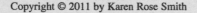

KAREN ROSE SMITH

is the award-winning, bestselling novelist of more than seventy published romances. Her latest miniseries, Reunion Brides, is set near Flagstaff, Arizona, in Miners Bluff, the fictional town she created. After visiting Flagstaff, the Grand Canyon and Sedona, Karen thought the scenery was so awe-inspiring that she had to set books there. When not writing, she likes to garden, growing herbs, vegetables and flowers. She lives with her husband—her college sweetheart—and their two cats in Pennsylvania. Readers may email her through her website at www.karenrosesmith.com or write to her at P.O. Box 1545, Hanover, PA 17331.

To Mike and M. R. Thanks for the inspiration.

Chapter One

Clay Sullivan strode into the cafeteria of his old high school. He hadn't even wanted to come to his fifteen-year reunion, yet he knew the confrontation he was going to have with Celeste Wells tonight was inevitable.

He hardly noticed the blue and yellow streamers that zigzagged across the ceiling, and ignored the classmates mingling and huddling around their old yearbooks. Catching sight of Celeste talking with a group of friends, a feeling of dread pulled tight across his chest.

Celeste rose when she saw him. Her light brown hair shimmered with highlights from the summer sun. The strapless white dress with pastel flowers decorating the full skirt showed off her creamy shoulders to perfection. She looked like his ex-wife—her fraternal twin sister—and at first glance he'd almost mistaken her for Zoie.

That was one mistake he couldn't afford to make.

"How are you?" Celeste asked as he approached her

table. Her wide green eyes showed compassion. Was that an act? Like the one Zoie had put on for so long?

"I'm here because you emailed that you wanted to see me," he responded, his voice gruff. "How long are you staying in Miners Bluff? Just tonight? Through the weekend?"

Celeste's cheeks flushed as she seemed to think over what she wanted to say.

Before she could answer him, music began to play at the other side of the room.

Celeste asked hopefully, "Do you want to go somewhere else and talk?"

He intended to keep this short and sweet. He didn't want to give Celeste an inch. He thought about his three-and-a-half-year-old daughter at home in her pj's, playing with her dollhouse. Abby was the sole reason he got up each morning. She was the last person he thought of before he went to sleep each night. Zoie had signed away her rights, and *he* had sole custody. That was the way it was going to stay.

"We can talk here. I don't think anyone's going to interrupt us." Not with the tension buzzing around them like a force field ready to singe anyone who came too close.

Celeste had always been the quiet, understated twin—in the way she dressed, the way she moved and the way she spoke. But now he saw something new come over her...something that put fire in those green eyes and a determined set to her pretty mouth.

She took a step closer to him, and the scent of honeysuckle titillated his senses. He wondered crazily if his large hands would span her slim waist. He stopped the thought before it had a chance to tickle his libido.

"Have you heard from Zoie recently?" she asked in a low voice.

He caught the note of worry and felt his heart soften a bit.

"Not since she signed the divorce papers a year ago. The last I heard she was traveling through France."

"You mean she hasn't contacted you at all about Abby?" Celeste sounded shocked, and he had to wonder if she *really* knew her sister.

"Are you so surprised? She's wanted to escape responsibility for a long time."

Celeste clasped his forearm in obvious sympathy and said softly, "Clay."

He felt unexpected heat on his skin, and he pulled away, startled by it. He and Celeste had never been more than friends. He shouldn't feel heat where she was concerned. "It's over, Celeste. I should have realized that before we had Abby."

He wanted to walk away, go back to his house in the foothills of Moonshadow Mountain where he could wall out everything but his daughter. Yet he couldn't look away from the compassion in Celeste's eyes. He couldn't look away from the understanding only she could have because she knew his history with Zoie from the beginning to the end—and she had played her own role in their drama.

Suddenly the music from the speakers blared louder. The DJ called, "Everybody find a partner."

Jenny Farber, one of the women Celeste had been conversing with when he'd walked in, came up to them and tapped both of their shoulders. "Come on, you two. Join in."

Clay had heard Jenny had helped organize this reunion. She was the manager of the Rocky D, a big spread outside of the town limits. He used their horses for his wilderness excursions. He liked Jenny and knew she was trying to lighten up the atmosphere between him and Celeste. But he doubted if anything could do that.

"Come on," Jenny encouraged them again. "It's nineties music at its best."

Maybe dancing with Celeste would throw her off her game…would divert her attention…would transport them into small talk instead of conversation about her and Abby.

"Do you want to dance?" he suggested. Yet as soon as he asked, the thought of holding Celeste in his arms made his gut clench. What had he gotten himself into?

As Celeste gazed at Clay's ruggedly chiseled face, his unruly dark brown hair, her stomach almost did backflips. He'd never known it, but he'd been her one and only crush until her extroverted sister had swept him away. Celeste hadn't had a chance. She'd made peace with that fact a long time ago. But tonight wasn't about the past. It was about her future with Abby.

"Sure, I'll dance with you," she answered, her heart racing because so much was on the line tonight.

When Clay's arm went around her, she felt as awkward as a teenager and wondered what was going through his head. Was he remembering the hikes they'd taken on Moonshadow Mountain before he'd dated Zoie? What about the after-school gatherings when chocolate milk was the beverage of choice? Even then, though, the zing had been between him and Zoie, and Celeste hadn't known how to make him really look at *her*.

He left enough space between them so she could look up and study his expression. But his steady gray eyes told her nothing. Tall and muscled, yet lean, his body so close to hers caused her throat to tighten and her mouth to go dry. Ever since Zoie's departure, Celeste had waited and waited and waited for a signal from Clay that he was ready for her to be a part of his daughter's life. But he hadn't given her one. So she'd planned to use this reunion as a stepping-stone to get to know the little girl.

"Who's with Abby tonight?" Celeste asked, hoping fireworks wouldn't erupt at that question.

"My mom."

That was a surprise. Violet Sullivan was a society matron, and the way she'd felt about Zoie, Celeste had been afraid she wouldn't take her granddaughter under her wing.

"Does she babysit often?"

"She watches Abby while I work."

Celeste apparently couldn't keep her surprise from showing because Clay added, "After Zoie left, she stepped right in. She said those young babysitters Zoie used didn't know the first thing about taking care of a child."

It was hard for Celeste to imagine Clay's mother as cuddly and warm. She'd always seemed so forbidding and proper, so against Clay's dating Zoie and hanging around with Celeste because they were from the wrong side of the tracks.

Silence fell over them as the music swelled, bringing back memories of high school dances, a ride home in Clay's car before he and Zoie left to spend time together, hours listening to music on her Walkman in her and Zoie's small bedroom above the bar where their mother worked.

Clay's arm tightened as a couple brushed past them. The dance floor seemed to shrink until there was just the two of them. Her breath caught and she knew she should push away. But the scent of Clay's cologne, the feel of his body against hers, created sensations she hadn't felt—hadn't let herself feel—for a very long time.

Clay's stubbled jaw tensed, and she expected him to put more space between them again, but he didn't. Instead, he asked, "Are you still working for that graphic design firm in Phoenix?"

Work. That should be easy to talk about. "No. I went out on my own and have a client list now. I create websites for businesses. Do you need one?" she asked teasingly.

"I've always been busy enough with word of mouth and ads in the right places that I didn't have to worry about that." He was a tour guide who led excursions around the area traveling mostly to nearby Flagstaff, north to the Grand Canyon, and south to Sedona. Miners Bluff, too, pulled in its share of sightseers who were curious about this former copper-mining town.

She guessed he wanted to lead the conversation away from Abby. But she wanted to dive right in while they were face-to-face. "Designing websites makes me portable. I can do it from anywhere. I don't have to live in Phoenix."

"Celeste..."

She heard the warning note in Clay's voice and knew she couldn't postpone the reason she'd come to the reunion any longer. "I want to see Abby. I want to spend time with her."

Clay's booted feet stopped moving for a moment.

They were still in the midst of dancing couples. Out of the corner of her eye, Celeste barely registered Mikala Conti dancing with Dawson Barrett, Riley O'Rourke smiling down at Brenna McDougall, Chief of Police Noah Stone leaning against the wall, watching them all.

After what seemed like eons—during which Celeste didn't know if Clay was going to break away or resume dancing—his hand tightened on hers, and he guided her away from the other dancers to a shadowed corner which, for the time being, was empty of classmates.

There he confronted her. "What do you want?"

The protective fierceness on his face should have scared her, but it didn't. This was Clay, the boy she'd known in high school, the young man who'd married her sister, the adult who had taken Zoie back after an affair, who'd tried to save his marriage by starting a family.

"I want to get to know Abby. I'd like to be a part of her life."

It was obvious Clay was greatly troubled by that idea and she suspected why.

She realized she had to give Clay a few minutes to think about her request. As they stood there close, yet not touching, she realized her attraction to Clay that had begun in high school had never gone away. She'd buried it as far down into her heart as she could. She'd never for a minute considered it would rise up to bite her now when she least expected it…now when she wanted Abby to be her only concern.

Finally Clay broke the silence between them. "All right." He checked his watch. "Abby might still be up. Why don't you come see that she's safe and loved? Then you can go back to Phoenix."

He was purposely misunderstanding what she wanted, which was to see Abby regularly. But she wasn't going to propose that now when he was giving her this opening.

"Let's go," she said before Clay could change his mind.

Clay was aware of the swish of Celeste's skirt as she preceded him up the lit walk to his house, a log home nestled among Douglas firs and aspen. He must have been certifiably crazy to ask her back here. Holding her in his arms, something had happened to him. Maybe because he hadn't been with a woman since before his separation and divorce, his body had responded to her. Whatever the reason, he'd felt an arousal he hadn't wanted to feel.

Perhaps she'd leave after this visit and his life would go back to the normal he was trying so hard to find.

"It's been a while since I've been here," she said with an almost shy smile as she glanced at him over her shoulder.

The motion caused her shawl to slip, and he automatically reached for it. As they'd left the school, the July night had turned cooler, and she'd slung the delicate, crocheted wrap around her. Every movement of Celeste's was graceful and natural. He'd always noticed that when they'd hiked. Zoie's movements had been more frenetic, some calculated to entice, others just meant to gain notice.

Clay lifted the end of the shawl over her shoulder. His hand brushed her hair, which felt as silky as it had looked when they were dancing. That same ripple of sensual awareness coursed through him again, and he mentally swore, frustrated with himself and the situation.

When Celeste's gaze met his, for a moment he forgot where he was. He forgot everything but the two of them standing there on the walk outside his house.

"I love the scent of the evergreens all around your property. And the petunias look lovely."

All he could smell now was the scent of Celeste's perfume. "Abby likes flowers so I asked Mom's gardener to plant a few. If we're lucky and the cold holds off, they could last through September."

"I don't miss the winter snow," Celeste said with a laugh. "But I do miss the green. I prefer firs to saguaros."

"Where are you staying while you're in Miners Bluff?"

"In one of the guest suites at Mikala's aunt's. The Purple Pansy Bed and Breakfast doesn't have a lot of rooms, but I think it's still one of the most hospitable places to stay in town."

"How is Ms. Conti?" He should have guessed Celeste would be staying near Mikala—one of her best friends from high school—but he thought at this time of year, the B and B might not have a vacancy.

"Anna doesn't seem to let anything get her down."

"I hear good things about Mikala's music therapy practice. I took a family sightseeing who'd driven up from Sedona so their daughter could spend a week in sessions with her."

"She never discusses her clients."

"No, but her clients discuss her, and you know how gossip makes the rounds in Miners Bluff."

"Oh, yes," Celeste murmured as they climbed the porch steps, then stood at his front door. "Quicker than a high-speed train."

Celeste's mother had been a target of the whispering chain around town. There had been rumors about her morals and the kind of life she'd led. She supposedly spent afternoon to midnight at the bar, drinking with the clientele, and slept with men who were patrons. She left her daughters alone too much of the time. Yet Clay knew rumors never told the whole truth. Clay had liked Ms. Wells. She'd raised Zoie and Celeste on her own the best she could. Her death when the twins were in their twenties had hit them both hard.

After Clay took out his key, he cast a glance at Celeste

and saw she was biting her lip. She was nervous. Nervous about not knowing what to expect with Abby? Or nervous about seeing his mother again? She'd spent Christmas with them all the year before Abby was born. She hadn't been back here since.

Clay opened the door, stepped back into the life he knew, the life he liked...the life he was satisfied with now.

Celeste was right behind him.

He realized little had changed from the way the house had looked a few years ago. He had exchanged the outlandishly colored sofa Zoie had wanted for a more muted blue plaid one. The gleaming hardwood floors, the dark rafters across the ceiling, the stone fireplace with its mantel, had remained the same.

"Great TV," Celeste joked with a smile.

He had to admit, yes, that was new, too. "Multipurpose. Not only does it allow Abby to watch her movies in almost life-size proportions, but I can run my footage of trips and wilderness treks, really seeing what I've got." He gave her a wink. "I could do my email on here, too, if I really wanted to."

She just shook her head. "I'm having trouble keeping up with technology and it's part of my business. Sometimes I wonder—"

A child's cry sounded down the left hall off the great room.

"Abby!" Clay called and hurried down the hall to the wing of bedrooms. In that moment, when his daughter needed him, he forgot about Celeste and why she'd come.

Clay's mom, who must have been sitting in the rocker reading—her book lay open on the chair—sat on Abby's canopy bed, holding her arms out to her granddaughter.

But Abby huddled near the pale pink wall, crying as if her heart were breaking.

"She had another bad dream," his mother said.

Abby had been having bad dreams on and off ever since Zoie had left two years ago. She couldn't possibly remember her mother, but he understood when a child's world changed, everything went topsy-turvy no matter how resilient they were supposed to be.

Clay crossed the room quickly, sat on the bed and gathered Abby into his arms. "Hey, ladybug. What's wrong?"

Abby shook her head and hiccupped, tears running down her chubby cheeks.

Out of the corner of his eye, he was aware of Celeste in the doorway. He saw his mother's frown and knew she was aware of her, too. He couldn't deal with Celeste now. In fact, he wished she'd leave.

But Celeste didn't leave. She looked uncertain—as if she might get thrown out—but she crossed the room slowly...as if she couldn't stay away. She knelt down before Abby and said in a soft voice, "That must have been a very bad dream. But your daddy's here now. He can protect you."

Abby glanced up to look at Clay, but then ducked her head down again, almost as if she were trying to crawl into herself. "Daddy's not always here."

"I'm here, honey, when your daddy's not." Violet Sullivan's voice sounded disappointed that her granddaughter didn't know that.

As if Celeste recognized that children didn't employ reason to come to a conclusion, she delved into Abby's world. "I'll bet your very favorite stuffed animal could protect you. I bet he could hold your hand all night if you wanted."

Sniffling, Abby peered up at Celeste. "Granny says I shouldn't sleep with my bears."

Clay glanced at his mother, then asked Abby, "Why is that?"

Abby explained, "She says they get dusty on the shelf."

Clay cleared his throat, unaware that conversation had ever happened. "If you think you'd like to sleep with one of your stuffed friends, we can make an exception tonight. Sometime soon maybe we can give them all a bath, then you'll be able to choose any one you want."

Abby removed her little arms from around her dad, swiped her wrist across her nose and studied Celeste for what seemed like an eternity. Then she squiggled to the edge of her pretty pink sheets and asked, "Will you come back and help me give them a baf?"

Clay could see that Celeste felt caught between what she wanted to do and what he might allow her to do. She answered, "I'll talk to your dad about that."

Abby just kept gazing into Celeste's face as if she were trying to figure something out. Clay knew what. This woman wasn't Zoie...but she was close.

Suddenly Abby held her arms out to Celeste, and without hesitation, Celeste took his little girl into her embrace. She sat on the edge of the bed, not far from Clay, and held Abby, her eyes shining with emotion, reverently brushing her long brown hair from her brow and cuddling her close.

The silence in the room seemed awkward to Clay, but Celeste and Abby didn't appear to notice. They were looking at each other again.

Suddenly Abby asked her, "Can you sing a song?"

When Celeste's gaze met Clay's, he gave a resigned shrug.

Tentatively at first, Celeste began singing a song about favorite things—roses and kittens—and Clay's stomach clenched. As Celeste's voice grew stronger, he realized it was the song Zoie had hummed to Abby after she was born. She hadn't sung it often, only on those rare times when she'd seemed to want to form a bond with her daughter. Did Abby remember? She wasn't saying whether she did or didn't. She was just cuddling into Celeste's body, letting herself be soothed and rocked, letting her eyes close.

After a short while, Celeste bent her head to Abby's and asked, "Do you think you're ready to go back to bed now, little one?"

His daughter nodded.

Sliding closer to Celeste, Clay was ready to take his daughter. But Abby shook her head and held on to Celeste tighter. Celeste looked puzzled as to what to do.

"Does she have a favorite toy?" Celeste asked him.

Abby's favorite toy. Did he even know which one that was? He'd been working so many hours lately, and she changed her mind every couple of months.

His mother's voice came from the rocker across the room. "Try that bear with the blue bow on the shelves. That seems to be her favorite lately."

Clay took it from the shelf and handed it to Abby. She tucked it under her arm.

Celeste asked, "Do you think you and your bear can go to sleep now?"

Abby's little hand settled on Celeste's cheek. Then she nodded and curled into a ball on the bed.

Oh, so gently, Celeste covered her with the sheet as Abby smiled sleepily, tucking the bear tighter into her side, then closed her eyes, gave a soft sigh and seemed to drift into sleep.

Celeste looked as if she never wanted to move.

Clay went to her and touched her elbow. She reluctantly

stood and accompanied him out of the room, but not until she glanced over her shoulder for a long last look at the sleeping child. His mother followed them into the great room, and once there the three adults seemed stymied as to where to begin. Clay could decipher the look in his mother's eyes that said she still didn't approve of the Wells twins, and she certainly didn't approve of Celeste coming here like this.

"It has been a long time, Celeste." Violet Sullivan patted her sedately coiffed ash-blond hair as if she needed *something* to do.

"Yes, it has," Celeste responded, still glancing down the hall to Abby's room. Then her full attention focused on his mother. "I haven't seen you since the Christmas before Abby was born. That was a wonderful holiday."

"Yes, it *seemed* to be."

Clay didn't like the censure in his mother's voice, didn't like the way it had been there all through his marriage to Zoie. Celeste, moreover, didn't deserve it. Just because his family had descended from the founding fathers of Miners Bluff, just because his family had always been well-off, was no reason for his mother to look down on Celeste—*especially* after what she'd done for him.

"Mom, could you sit with Abby while Celeste and I talk? She might wake up again."

After a long worried look, his mother returned to his daughter.

"Let's go outside," he said gruffly to Celeste, and headed for the front door. He knew what had just happened between Abby and Celeste had to be addressed and addressed now.

Because Celeste Wells was more than a concerned aunt.

She was Abby's surrogate mother.

Chapter Two

Outside on Clay's front porch, a motherly fervor rose up in Celeste she'd never experienced before. If Clay thought she was going to walk away from her daughter this time, he was wrong. Even though his sperm and Zoic's egg had made Abby, Celeste had felt a motherly bond from the moment of conception, though she'd denied it for years.

She squared her shoulders and met Clay's turmoiled gaze head-on. "After Abby was born, it practically broke my heart to give her to you and Zoie. But that's what I'd promised to do. I know I signed release forms and still don't have any rights. But having rights and doing what's right are two different things. You're her father and you have sole custody. I understand that. But I carried her for thirty-eight and a half weeks. I felt her move inside me. I looked into her little face after she was born and felt... connected. I came back here to get to know her, to spend some time with her, and I hope you're compassionate enough to understand why I have to do that."

Clay didn't look moved and his silence troubled her. So she asked, "How often does Abby have bad dreams?" Celeste remembered the feel of her daughter in her arms. Abby had looked up at her as if she'd known her!

Finally Clay reluctantly admitted, "Every few weeks. She hasn't had one for a while." He ran his hand through his shaggy dark hair. "I talked to her pediatrician about them but he believes they'll pass."

Clay's eminent virility was difficult to ignore. And the regret in his voice tugged at her heart. Still, she probed for more information. "The dreams will pass when Abby feels secure again?"

"She *is* secure," Clay assured her firmly. "She's a happy little girl."

"Until she goes to sleep at night...until she plays with other children and realizes she doesn't have a mommy," Celeste pointed out, unwilling to let this go.

"She was too young to remember Zoie. She was only eighteen months when Zoie and I separated."

"Zoie came back to get the divorce a year later," Celeste reminded him.

"She didn't stay with us," he protested. "She and I met at the lawyer's office and she only saw Abby once."

Celeste could clearly see on his face the turmoil her visit had caused. "Abby looked at me as if she knows me. She remembers Zoie."

Swearing under his breath, Clay swung away from her and stared into the dark night, the mountains and the sky above. Finally he asked again with resignation, "What do you want?"

She wondered if he thought this time her answer would

be different…if her answer would let him go back to the life he'd been leading before her email.

"For now, I'd just be happy to spend some time with Abby under ordinary circumstances."

Clay came a couple of paces closer, the intensity in his eyes edging his words. "What's this going to be, Celeste? You'll be here a week then go back to your life in Phoenix? You want to spend holidays now and then with Abby? You intend to be a favorite aunt and come in and out of her life as it suits you?"

Celeste was stung by Clay's anger, though deep down she knew some of it was justified. He'd been hurt by the divorce. He'd ridden out his turbulent marriage, tried to do the right thing and ended up as a single dad with a child to raise on his own. How could she tell him what she wanted when she didn't know herself? She'd been hurt by love, too, not so long ago. But one thing was certain—she wanted a place in Abby's life.

For a few moments, Clay's closeness stole her breath. She remembered the strength of his fingers around hers as they'd danced, his hand splayed across the small of her back, the musk-and-pine scent of him that now stirred a sleepy need inside her.

Gathering her wits, reclaiming her senses, she tried to detach herself from Clay, the man, to talk to Clay, the father. "I'm here to stay if that's what will be best for Abby."

Shock deepened the brackets around his mouth, the lines at his eyes. "You're willing to commit to staying in Miners Bluff to watch Abby grow up?" His voice held wariness and disbelief.

But Celeste had already spent many sleepless nights deciding what to do. "Yes. I think of her as my daughter.

But I won't disrupt her life and I'll do what's best for her."

Clay was shaking his head, widening his stance. "You've got to give me some time to think about this, to figure out the best way to handle it."

Trying to let him absorb her intention, she pulled a folded piece of paper from her purse. "My cell phone number's on there as well as my number at Mikala's. I'll be waiting for your call."

When she handed him the slip of paper, their fingers brushed. Awareness rushed through her and the flicker in his eyes told her something jarred him a little, too. High school memories? A history they couldn't refute? The way their lives were converging once more?

As Celeste descended Clay's porch steps, she remembered how she and her mother had watched movies together when she was a teenager and Zoie was out with friends. Her favorite movie had been *Raiders of the Lost Ark*. Clay had always reminded her of Indiana Jones—intelligent, adventurous and too sexy for words.

Now as she made her way to her car, she felt his gaze burning through her back.

The disco ball was still spinning when Celeste returned to the cafeteria where the reunion was in full swing. When Mikala waved at her, she headed to join her friend, who was sitting alone.

"You disappeared," Mikala said, pushing her wavy black hair behind one ear.

Easily settling into the years-old routine of confiding in her old friend, she revealed, "I saw Abby. I actually held her." She stopped when she heard the tremor in her voice, knowing she was already caring too much. If Clay wanted her gone, she'd really have no right to stay, so she couldn't let herself get too attached.

Mikala didn't seem to need her to say more. They sat listening to the music for a few moments.

Celeste's thoughts raced as she tried to find a distraction. This reunion wasn't over tonight. In the summer, the chamber of commerce scheduled rodeos for alternate Sundays, so some classmates planned to attend the event at the fairgrounds tomorrow. Maybe Clay would be there?

So much for a distraction. "Are you going to the rodeo tomorrow?"

"I'll go if Aunt Anna doesn't need me. The family staying in our other suite is checking out tomorrow morning."

The Purple Pansy only had two suites, but Celeste knew Mikala didn't want her aunt to carry the entire burden.

"I saw you dancing with Dawson Barrett before I left," Celeste noted just in case her friend wanted to confide in *her*.

Mikala's gaze went to the tall man in question who was embroiled in a lively conversation with a group of classmates.

"Is he still CEO of his own company?" Celeste asked, knowing Dawson also lived in Phoenix.

"You don't run in the same circles?" Mikala asked with a smile.

Celeste laughed. "Oh, no. I think he's in the millionaire club. And Phoenix is way too big for me to run into him by accident. But I read about what happened to his wife. He has a son, doesn't he?"

Mikala's face suddenly took on her professional look, and Celeste knew what that meant. She was a stickler for confidentiality in her practice. Had Dawson talked to her about his son?

Even if Mikala wanted to, she didn't get the opportunity to answer. They both heard raised voices coming from a corridor that led off the cafeteria to the stairway beyond.

"That's Jenny," Celeste said, rising to her feet.

Mikala put a hand on Celeste's arm. "She and Zack Decker stepped out there for a private conversation. He arrived shortly after you left. No one thought he'd come, since he hasn't been back to see his father at the Rocky D in years. I guess everyone expected him to drive up in a limo or something. But even with that Oscar for film directing under his belt, he acted like a regular guy."

Just then Jenny and Zack emerged from the corridor, both looking angry. Zack headed out of the cafeteria towards the school's lobby. Jenny headed in the opposite direction, toward the ladies' room.

"We should see if she's okay," Celeste said, well aware Jenny and Zack had been involved their senior year of high school.

"Let's give her a few minutes. If she doesn't come out, we'll go in."

Celeste sank down onto her folding chair again, trying to decide if reunions were a good thing or a bad thing. Old friends reconnected. The night brought back memories everyone had forgotten. Yet being together with classmates in this room stirred up old hurts, too... as well as old hopes.

Don't go there. Old dreams were just that—old dreams. She'd returned to Miners Bluff to find new ones.

Celeste had always loved the rodeo. The scent of french fries and hot dogs, burgers and barbecued chicken wings reminded her of the times she'd come here as a teenager. Along with hiking on Moonshadow Mountain, she'd attended the rodeo on summer Sundays looking for an escape from everyday life, from gossip about her mother, from the sounds of raucous laughter that had drifted up from the bar—The Tin Pan Tavern—underneath her bedroom almost every night. When she'd earned enough money as a cashier at the grocery store to buy a rodeo ticket, she'd thrown herself into the experience, cheering on the clowns and the riders, eating fries sprinkled with vinegar, pretending for a few hours that she was an adult, free to do whatever she pleased.

Little had she known that adults had restrictions, too.

Behind her, Jenny followed her into the stands, waving at several people she knew. Celeste smiled at classmates who'd hung around for this event and found a seat near some of them.

Not long after she and Jenny were seated, a lone rider trotted from the gate behind the arena, a flag held high. Everyone stood as the "Star Spangled Banner" played

A cheer went up from the crowd as the first event commenced and women's barrel racing captured Celeste's attention…

Until a deep male voice asked, "Is this seat taken?"

She'd know that voice anywhere. Before she turned to face Clay, she took a deep breath and reminded herself he was Abby's father, nothing more.

Yet as she turned her face up to him and gazed into his gunmetal-gray eyes, she felt herself falling again into memories of another time when she'd wanted Clay to notice *her,* not her twin.

"Hey," she said with a flippancy she wasn't feeling. "I didn't know you liked rodeos."

"I've developed a taste for them."

"You didn't think much of them when we were in high school." Zoie and Clay's dates had never brought them here.

"Not true. My parents are the ones who don't think much of them, and…"

"And Zoie wasn't crazy about them, either."

"No. She preferred driving into Flagstaff or Sedona to window-shop. But *you* loved the summer rodeo cycle."

She was surprised he knew that. "I sure did. Still do. But I'm usually too busy to take time to enjoy one in Phoenix."

"How did we ever become adults who don't have time for fun?"

His tone shifted, and she could see he was serious.

After Clay settled in beside her, his arm brushing hers, she took another long breath, warning herself to stay calm. But she was nervous about Clay approaching her. What did it mean?

They watched horse and rider expertly circle the barrels, ending the competition with a gallop toward the finish line. A rousing cheer went up around them.

When the audience calmed down and the next rider approached the first barrel, Clay leaned toward her. "Do you want to find a quieter place to talk?"

She glanced at Jenny, who was deep in conversation with someone seated behind her. "Sure."

"We can get something to drink," he said as if they needed an excuse for leaving the stands.

She bent to Jenny. "We're going to get drinks. Would you like me to bring you back anything?"

Jenny just looked at Clay and shook her head. "I'll go down in a little while. Don't hurry back on my account."

Celeste wasn't sure what to make of Jenny's remark, but she followed Clay down to the ground and strode behind him until he stopped, waiting for her. "Iced tea or soda?"

"Iced tea. Unsweetened if they have it."

After he bought them drinks, they wandered along a row of stalls until they reached a clearing behind the corrals. Riders practiced roping there. Colorfully dressed clowns passed them. A man Clay knew waved as he led a horse down the walkway.

"I should have handled last night differently." Clay pushed up the brim of the crushable fedora that he wore most of the time when he wasn't inside. In that hat, with its wide brim, pinched sides and dented top, he again reminded her of Indiana Jones.

"Differently how?"

"We were friends once, Celeste. I never intended to treat you like the enemy."

She released a huge pent-up breath, but then she realized he might be trying to lessen the tension between them so she'd back off. She'd told him she had Abby's best interests at heart. Maybe he thought if he was friendly enough, he could convince her that staying out of Abby's life would be the best thing for his daughter. Then he wouldn't have to deal with her.

She didn't accept his olive branch so easily. "We don't know each other anymore."

"No, we don't." As his gaze studied her, a tremor went up and down her spine, not because he could keep her out of Abby's life, but because she was still attracted to him. Attracted to him in a way she shouldn't be if she didn't want to get hurt again. She watched a flicker of... something pass over his face.

Then his jaw tightened, and his spine became more rigid. "What would it take to get you to leave?"

Instead of answering him, she asked, "Don't you think having a female role model around might be good for Abby?"

"And just how do I explain you, Celeste? Do I tell her you're her aunt? Or do I tell her you're sort of her mother but she has another mother who didn't *want* to be her mother and ran away from every responsibility she professed she was ready for?"

Celeste had been aware of how unhappy Zoie had been, as well as the reasons why. Did Clay even know what they were? He probably didn't care. He was still raw from her desertion.

Taking a step away from Clay out of the virile aura he exuded, she said, "Maybe you should stop thinking about all the possible questions you have and just listen to me. I don't want to hurt Abby. I want to be around for her. I understand you want to protect her, but did you ever think she might need me in her life with Zoie gone?"

With a stoic expression, Clay contemplated the nearby cowboy twirling his rope above his head. Then he refocused all his attention on her. "You never used to be this tenacious." He sounded as if he might respect and admire that quality now.

"I didn't have a reason to be tenacious." After a few moments, she added, "You never looked beyond who I was in high school."

He shrugged, one hand slipping into the back pocket of his jeans. "You were always quiet and seemed to hold back."

"I stood in my sister's shadow?" she prompted, knowing she hadn't fought then to escape Zoie's vibrant personality.

"Your words, not mine."

"That doesn't mean they're not true. I found a life after I left Miners Bluff, a life that gave me confidence in my own abilities and in what I could accomplish." She should have added, "In who I was as a woman," but she didn't want to get into that. Her personality had always been swallowed up by Zoie's.

The late afternoon sun streamed down on them as applause rose once more from the crowd in the stands.

The one thing Celeste had learned to do was to be honest about what she wanted and what she was feeling. She kept her voice low but didn't hesitate to make eye contact. "Do you know what I felt last night, Clay, when Abby held on to me?"

He stepped nearer to her so it was easier to hear, so no one else could hear. "What?"

His mouth was close to her ear. His breath was warm. A quiver slid down her spine, and she fought attraction she had to deny. "I felt as if she was part of me, the same way I felt when she was still inside me. For over three years I've denied how I felt that day. I've denied the yearnings that brought me back here."

He was still so close to her, his body heat was converging with hers when he asked, "What finally brought you back? I can't believe the reunion was the reason you emailed me."

"No, it wasn't." But she was sure he didn't want to hear about a failed relationship, didn't want to hear how she'd thought she'd found a man to love but then he'd rejected her in the most obvious of ways. She'd been blind and would try never to be so again.

"The reason doesn't matter. I had to see Abby. I think she and I might need each other."

It was easy to see that Clay cared about what his

daughter needed, even if he wasn't thrilled about Celeste's potential involvement in her life. "I don't have any tours tomorrow. Come over to the house around four. She should be up from her nap by then if she takes one. I'll tell her I've invited you to her tea party. She has one almost every afternoon. Mom started it as a prelude to dinner so she'd eat some fruit and veggies." He hesitated. "You know, Abby asked me this morning if you could visit again."

Celeste forgot about the barrel racers, the applause, the aroma of burgers and fries. So *that* was the reason he'd offered an olive branch.

As she lifted her chin, Clay's lips were within kissing distance. She spoke past the lump in her throat. "You won't regret this, Clay."

Judging by his expression, he clearly didn't believe her.

Clay forced a smile when he opened the door to Celeste the following day. At the rodeo, he'd felt that disorienting tug of attraction again. His body had responded to her with startling insistence—and he didn't like it. He'd always been a master of self-control—why was his body overruling his head?

Celeste was carrying a two-foot-high plush calico cat. He commented amiably, "You brought a friend."

"For Abby."

"To keep away her nightmares?" he guessed, realizing there was a point to everything Celeste did.

"Possibly. If not, just another friend to enjoy the tea party."

"Up until now, only bears were invited," he said conversationally, leading her toward the sunroom at the back of the house. "But I think she'll make an exception." He added, "Mom's still here. She stayed with Abby while I ran errands. Abby asked her to stay for snacks with you." When he glanced over at Celeste, he saw she hadn't reacted to that news.

They entered the bright space with its floor-to-ceiling screened windows on two walls. His mother sat beside Abby on the floor, a porcelain tea set atop a white wooden table. There were fresh vegetables and fruit along with milk in the teapot.

Celeste didn't hesitate to approach his mother and Abby. "Hello, Mrs. Sullivan. It's good to see you again."

His mother simply nodded in response.

With the lift of a brow, Celeste crouched beside Abby. "Hi, Abby. Do you remember me?"

His daughter smiled and nodded, too, not acting shy as she usually did with people she didn't know well.

"Well, good, I'm glad you do. I brought someone along today who would like to meet you. Her name is Tulullah. Tulullah, meet Abby."

Abby's grin was so wide, Clay felt a tug at his heart. "Tooloo," she tried to say.

"Maybe we could just call her Lulu," Celeste suggested.

"I like Lulu," Abby decided, looking over the cat and making room for it to sit on the floor.

Celeste's gaze found Clay's, and he felt his pulse thump in his jaw. Determined to ignore the flash of heat, he lowered himself to the floor beside Celeste, his jean-clad thigh brushing hers as they settled in. Another jolt of adrenaline rushed through him that caused even more turmoil.

She shifted away, and he told himself he was glad. This was *not* the time for his libido to wake up after two years of dormancy.

"Would you like me to pour?" she asked Clay's mother.

"That would be fine," his mother answered formally.

He found himself watching Celeste much too closely. After she poured the milk, she took a sip from her cup, licked her lips, and set it on the table. Zoie would have done all that provocatively and on purpose. Celeste... He could see she was just enjoying spending time with Abby.

"Do you know how long you'll be staying in Miners Bluff?" his mother asked.

Abby suddenly stood, ran to her toy bin in the corner and produced a hat with ribbon ties. Sidling up to Celeste, she asked, "Can you put it on Lulu? I can't tie."

"Of course I can," Celeste said, taking the hat from Abby. Then she answered Violet. "How long I stay depends on all of you."

His mom looked surprised at the answer.

"She looks beautiful," Celeste decreed, as the big pink bow flopped under Lulu's chin. "That hat was a good idea."

Abby looked at Lulu, back at Celeste, then threw her arms around Celeste's neck. "I *like* Lulu. I like you. T'ank you."

Clay watched Celeste's eyes close and her lower lip tremble. "You're most welcome."

Wiggling in again between Celeste and Lulu, Abby thoughtfully took a bite of strawberry. Then she tugged Celeste's arm. "Can you play puzzles wif me?"

Celeste looked at Clay as if for permission.

He pointed to a stack of toddler puzzles on the bookshelf, but warned his daughter, "Celeste might have to go back to her own house. It's getting near suppertime."

"Can she have supper wif us? And wash my bears?" Abby asked innocently.

This he hadn't expected.

"If you have other plans, Abby will understand," his mother assured her, as if she wanted her to go. In fact, she got to her feet as if to signal the tea party was over.

But Clay had to find out what Celeste was made of. He had to find out if she belonged in his daughter's life.

"You're welcome to stay," he said gruffly, wanting to see what decision she would make.

She didn't hesitate. "I'd like to. But please let me help with dinner. I don't want you to go to any trouble."

"Do you cook?" his mother asked her.

"I do. It's a hobby."

Clay's mother frowned. "Well, you're certainly very different from your sister. She preferred takeout, restaurants, or else a personal chef."

"Mom," Clay said in warning.

His mother eyed Celeste again. "I have to be going. Harold will be waiting for me." She gave Abby a hug and a kiss. "I'll see you tomorrow, honey."

After an even longer look at Celeste, she said in a low voice to Clay, "I'll tell your father you're going to consider his ideas for your retirement account."

"No, Mom. I'm *not*."

"Humor him," she coaxed.

Clay sighed. "I'll speak to him about the account, but I don't intend to change anything."

"At least that's something," his mother murmured, squeezed his shoulder and then left the sunroom.

Although Celeste was already putting a puzzle together with Abby, she tossed him a quizzical look.

"I know what you're thinking," he said.

"I'm not thinking anything, except maybe your dad still wants you to be a banker."

His father had always wanted him to be a banker... just as Zoie had. "Some things never change."

"Doesn't he accept the fact that you're doing the work you love? Doesn't that matter to him at all?"

So Celeste had always realized that. The revelation settled into Clay's being as if it was important enough to make a home there. "My father isn't interested in the journey. He's always been interested in appearances and the end result. He wants me to be a respected member of the community and take over for him some day."

"Turn the puzzle piece this way," Celeste encouraged Abby. "There you go. That one fits."

Abby clapped her hands and hugged Lulu tighter against her. "It fits, Lulu!"

As Abby selected another piece with Cinderella's fairy godmother stamped on it, Celeste asked Clay, "Do you still *like* what you do? Do you still want to get into that SUV and drive where not many people go, hike where few people dare, teach others about the beauty of this place?"

He heard passion in Celeste's voice. He'd never thought of her as passionate. That had been Zoie's forte. "Yes, or I wouldn't still be doing it." He leaned around Celeste to tug on one of his daughter's pigtails.

She grinned at him. "Don't tease, Daddy."

He laughed. He knew in spite of everything, Abby was the best thing that had ever happened to him. And whether he wanted to acknowledge it or not, he had Celeste to thank for that.

Levering himself up to a sitting position again, his chest brushed Celeste's shoulder. She glanced back at him and he studied her face. His first impression at the reunion had been wrong—she did look a bit like Zoie, but not as much as he'd thought. Her perfume was different, her gaze was, too. It was direct, not evasive. In that moment, he wondered what it would be like to kiss her—if her lips would be soft and pliant, if passion would be natural for her or a means to get what she wanted.

Abby.

He pushed himself to his feet. "We're having turkey burgers tonight. I'll turn on the grill and set up a washbasin outside because I'm sure the bears' bath will get messy."

"Can I wear my swimsuit?" Abby asked, scrambling to her feet.

He tried to let the tension he felt with Celeste ease away so his daughter wouldn't pick up on it. "Sure."

Celeste turned away and took a deep breath. Was she feeling chemistry, too? Why now?

Rising to her feet, she asked, "What can I do to help?"

All of a sudden, he imagined the two of them naked and tangled in each other's arms. Where the hell had *that* vision come from? That rush of adrenaline that still lingered? The bite of arousal he'd relegated to a remnant of younger days?

No, he could *not* get involved with this woman. Or any woman. His nine-year marriage had drained all the romance out of him. Zoie's betrayal had left him distrustful at worst…guarded at best. Why would he want to risk that kind of pain again? Why would he put Abby at risk of getting hurt, too?

Coolly he said, "The washbasin is in the laundry room. Towels, too. Maybe you can bring those outside."

"Can C'leste help me put on my swimsuit?"

Clay's heart took a nosedive. Already Abby was bonding with Celeste. He had to make a decision whether he should let it happen or stop it right now.

What would be best for his daughter—and for *him?*

Chapter Three

Celeste paced Clay's sunroom, anxiety making her nauseous. Had she passed the test? Would he think she was good for his daughter?

Her daughter, she reminded herself. *Her* daughter.

They'd washed the toys and then enjoyed a pleasant supper on the patio. At least *she* thought it had been pleasant.

Until her gaze had met Clay's and something electric had filled the air.

He'd turned away. She'd turned away. They'd both *moved* away, never getting within touching distance as they played tag with Abby and hide-and-seek and a funny little game Abby had produced with a blue elephant and butterflies.

But Clay hadn't invited her to participate in the bedtime ritual. He'd said that she could go inside, relax and watch TV if she wanted.

But she couldn't relax. Not waiting for his judgment call. She felt as if tonight her life could change forever. And she preferred the shadows of the sun porch to the glare of the great-room lights.

She heard Clay's footsteps as he strode through the kitchen. Only the summer moon cut a swath of light across the yard as Clay's voice preceded him into the sunroom. "Celeste?"

"I'm here. I was listening to the sounds—the owls, the breeze in the leaves. Most of all I like the scents—the pines and the sage."

His voice was a deep rumble in the shadows. "I've centered my life around the scents, the sounds, the textures of the landscape."

She wished he'd step into the moonlight so she could see his expression. "You made a life around it. During my life I made memories of it. As soon as I was old enough, I ran up these mountains to escape the noise of the bar and Mom bringing men home. Those sensory memories will always be a part of me, just as holding Abby in my arms for the first time will be, remembering the warmth and softness of her skin."

Now he took a step into her space, right into the glow of the moon. If he wanted her to step back, she didn't. She could see the silver flecks in Clay's eyes, almost feel the muscled fitness of his body. The heat of the July day was almost gone now, yet she could feel heat between them. Maybe that was just on her part.

"Are you trying to convince me of something?" he asked roughly.

"No. I've just told you how I feel."

He swore, turned away, then faced her again, the tension in his body so evident that she could practically feel the sensual ripples.

"Clay." She said his name so softly it was almost a whisper.

"Don't," he ordered.

"Don't what?"

"Don't look at me as if you want to be more than Abby's mother. Don't you get it, Celeste? I'm *feeling,* too."

She knew if she asked the next question, she might not like the answer. But she asked anyway. "What are you feeling?"

He seemed to struggle with what he wanted to say and how he wanted to say it. "I'm attracted to you. I can't get you out of my mind. Sure, it's part worry about you and Abby. But so much of it is just..." He stopped to study her...to assess how she might react. "So much of it is raw desire that's making me crazy!"

She knew she could run. That's probably what he expected her to do. Instead, she stood her ground because this was Clay—a boy she'd fallen hard for, a man she now desired. So she said, "I dream about you, too."

Her words seemed to break a wall between them. He reached out and touched her face. His fingers were scorching. She didn't breathe.

His groan was low as his arms encircled her and his lips came down on hers. Her breath became trapped in her chest as she kissed him back, bringing her hands to his shoulders, gripping him tightly so her knees wouldn't buckle.

She heard his deep groan, felt his desire ratchet up as his tongue parted her lips, and he claimed her more possessively. She'd imagined this moment when she was in high school, yet she'd never expected it to happen. Once Zoie and Clay were dating steadily, she'd locked all her feelings tightly in a corner of her heart, never intending to let them show, never intending to act on them, never intending to let Clay see them.

As he pressed his body against hers, she felt herself melting into him, fitting against him as if this kiss was going to go a lot further. Clay rubbed against her, explored her mouth more thoroughly, took the kiss into the realm of deep passion instead of skimming the surface of their desire.

But just as suddenly as they'd come together, he pulled away and took a long, deep breath. "That never should have happened. Ever since you came back..." He abruptly stopped and shook his head. "You look like Zoie, yet you don't. And you're different than she was. You're passionate and so natural with Abby. I don't know if I'm attracted to you or if this is just some kind of libido-memory thing."

Could he possibly know how much that hurt her? To be compared to Zoie and brushed aside as if she weren't capable of inciting a man's desire?

Even in the dim light, he must have seen the emotion on her face because he clasped her arm and said, "I didn't mean that the way it came out."

"Maybe you did. Maybe this has nothing to do with me at all."

He seemed to consider that and then shook his head. "No. Ever since we danced, there's this...*buzz* between us. You obviously feel it, too, or you would have backed away. Why didn't you?"

Now *he* was the one who wanted answers, yet she couldn't give them. She realized now she didn't want to reveal too much. Knowledge was power, and he could use that knowledge and power in all sorts of ways. She didn't think he would, but as protective as he was of Abby, he might not take any chances by giving her even a little bit of leeway.

When she didn't answer him, he concluded, "We have to ignore it." His words were filled with conviction. "Chemistry will only complicate our lives even more. It was all Zoie and I had when we started and we didn't even have that when we finished."

There was a world of pain in that admission, pain from giving his life to someone and having her tear it up. She knew about that, but not as much as Clay did.

"Have you dated since the divorce?" she asked quietly.

He rubbed the back of his neck and shook his head. "Celeste, there's no reason to get into this."

"I'd like to know if there have been any other women in Abby's life." *And in yours.*

"I wouldn't have brought a woman into Abby's life, not unless I was absolutely sure she'd be committed to staying in it. So, no, I haven't dated."

That summed up the intensity of the kiss for Celeste. If he hadn't been with a woman, it would be easy for his desire to blaze out of control.

His voice was gruff as he lifted her chin and gazed into her eyes. "I can't say that what you're thinking isn't wrong."

Another zinger. He could read her mind. That was almost as scary as the fact that he might have kissed her simply because she reminded him of Zoie.

"Are *you* seeing anyone?" he asked, dropping his hand. "Are you involved in Phoenix?"

There was suspicion in his eyes, a remnant from Zoie's betrayal. "I wouldn't have kissed you if I was."

She hoped that was true. But all those old longings had coalesced into a passionate encounter she wouldn't soon forget. If one of his kisses could shake her up that much, heaven help her if they went further than that.

But he wouldn't—because of Abby. Because he didn't want to stir up a hornet's nest.

"Tonight was a test run, wasn't it?" she asked.

"You mean with Abby?"

"Yes." What else would she mean, unless— "Did you kiss me to see what I would do to get access to Abby? Was that the test, too?"

"Don't make more of it than it was, Celeste. I have to know what you're planning to do now."

"I'm serious about moving here, Clay. The question is—how often will you let me see her?"

He raked his fingers through his hair, glanced toward Abby's bedroom, then said, "Let's start with a couple of visits a week for now. My mother will be here while you're with her. Is that acceptable to you?"

He sounded as if he were setting up a legal agreement.

"That's fine. I hope in time you'll trust me with her alone."

"I don't have an abundance of trust right now."

The truth of that statement was as evident as the fine lines around his eyes, the tension in his jaw, the defensiveness in his stance. She wanted to break through the walls he'd constructed after Zoie had left.

Maybe in time, he'd learn she *wasn't* like her sister.

"I shouldn't have come to this cocktail party," Celeste said to Jenny on Friday evening as her friend ushered her into Silas Decker's huge house. Zack's father bred and trained cutting horses, turning over more of the management of the Rocky D ranch to Jenny every year.

When Jenny was a teenager, she'd come to live and

work at the Rocky D. But to Silas she'd come to be much more than an employee. She was the daughter he'd never had.

"If Silas is introducing Clay to friends who want a fishing guide, I don't want to intrude." The more she thought about seeing Clay again, the more nervous she'd become.

Jenny was having none of that. "He's doing that, but we're watching Zack's new movie, too. You're my friend, and I want you here. As I told you on the phone, Silas is trying to fix me up again. I don't want to be fixed up. I'm happy here doing what I'm doing, and doing it without worrying about what some man's going to think of me."

Celeste thought Jenny was protesting a little too much. She wondered again about the argument she'd had with Zack the night of the reunion. She hadn't wanted to talk about it. They'd been quite an item their senior year, and from their angry parting, there still seemed to be some heat between them.

"Did you hear from Zack after the reunion?"

A mutinous expression flamed on Jenny's face. "I don't want to hear from Zack, not unless he's telling me he's coming home to figure out how to lessen the load on his dad."

"Is there a problem?"

Jenny didn't respond for a few moments, as if considering the facts, and whether she should or shouldn't say anything about them. "I've seen some changes in the last couple of months. Silas's energy's definitely lower. He needs to rest more. He doesn't have the verve he used to when he's working in the barns. And with the book work, he could care less. He used to be on top of *all* of it. I asked him to consider going to the doctor for a checkup, but he said he's fine. My instincts are telling me something's going on."

"What does Zack think?"

"He thinks I'm overreacting. But he was here less than twenty-four hours. How could he tell?"

"That's why you argued?"

"Yes. And now I'm going to forget about it and just keep pushing Silas to see his physician." She let out a deep breath. "So tell me what's happening with you and Clay and Abby."

Celeste felt warmth creep up her neck, and Jenny noticed.

"Well?" she asked, one hand on her hip, slightly wrinkling her coral sheath, her blond head cocked, her brown eyes penetrating.

"I saw Abby last Sunday and again on Monday when Clay was there. Then I visited again yesterday and he wasn't there. His mother was."

"How did that go?"

"It went okay, actually. His mom doesn't seem to know what to think of me, though. She expects me to be flighty...like Zoie."

Jenny brought a finger to her chin, then gave a slight nod as if she'd settled something with herself. "I never told you, but I saw Zoie once with Abby when she was about six months old. She had her in a grocery cart, pushing her around the store. The thing was—she didn't pay much attention to her. When Abby fussed, she just let her fuss and kept shopping as if nothing was happening. This was one time and it might not have meant anything at all. She might have been tired. Maybe Abby had been fussing all day. But I wondered if that was the way she treated her all the time. It was none of my business, so I kept out of it. But I wondered."

"If you had told me, I would have come back sooner."

"And then what?"

Wasn't that a loaded question? Would she have barged into Zoie and Clay's life, claimed her daughter wasn't getting the attention and love she needed? Wasn't that why she'd chosen to make a life for herself in Phoenix, so she wouldn't interfere, wouldn't see, wouldn't be involved?

"Come on," Jenny said, hooking her arm in Celeste's. "Let's join the party. Silas's out-of-town friends heard about Clay and his tours and wanted to meet him in person. Silas also invited Jesse Vargas, Brody Hazlett and his dad, so you won't be stuck in a room with Clay all night. Besides, I need a little girl company."

Jenny led Celeste across the marble foyer, through a covered archway that opened into a high-ceilinged living room with a Remington on the wall, cowhide rugs and a suede and leather sofa long enough for a giant.

"Everyone's in Silas's parlor. Martha's serving appetizers and drinks. You're the last to arrive."

Great, Celeste thought. That meant everyone would notice her when they walked in. She reminded herself she was no longer a shy teenager who preferred back corners to dancing under the spotlight. Holding her head high, she straightened to her full height, glad she'd worn heels instead of sandals, glad her teal dress, which had been an alternate choice for the reunion, had been a recent purchase before her trip here.

Celeste felt as if she should knock on the mahogany French doors that led into the parlor, but Jenny didn't hesitate to grab a glass knob and open one of them. For a few moments, masculine voices circled around the group in the center of the room. Celeste recognized one deep baritone right away, but she kept her gaze from swinging to Clay. Instead she focused on the man at the center of the circle. He'd lost most of his gray hair, but his gray-black mustache seemed as thick as ever. The multitude of lines on his face attested to the fact that he'd aged since Celeste had seen him last.

"He *has* changed," Celeste whispered to Jenny.

"In a lot of ways. Most of all, I think he's just sad that he and Zack can't talk."

After only a few moments of hesitation, Celeste decided. "We might as well dive right in." She tried to come up with a genuine smile.

"*You've* changed, too," Jenny muttered as side by side they approached the closed group.

All of a sudden, one of the men Celeste didn't know gave a low whistle and slapped Silas Decker on the back. "Where have you been keeping these two lovely ladies?"

Silas shrugged off the thirty-something man's hand and turned to greet them. "Jenny, I'm so glad you invited Celeste." He held her hand and then kissed the top of it lightly. "You've grown into quite a beauty."

"Thank you. I don't want to interrupt your conversation."

"As usual, we were talking horses. Clay was trying to explain to us why he picks the ones he does when he goes on trail rides. You were always a good picker, too, when you and Jenny convinced me to let you ride up to Moonshadow or out to Feather Peak. How do *you* choose?"

"It's not very scientific," she joked. "I look into his eyes, see if he likes my touch or pulls away from it. I give him a few ground commands and see how well he obeys. Then I take him for a little walk to get a feel for rhythm and companionability."

Several men cleared their throats. Brody, a veterinarian

like his dad, asked, "You don't listen to recommendations from others?"

"I've learned recommendations from others don't go very far if the horse and I don't understand the same language."

"Do you pick your dates that way?" Silas joked.

Unoffended, she shot back, "Maybe I should."

The majority of the group laughed, but with one glance at Clay, she could see he wasn't one of them. Even with that quick meeting of their eyes, she could still feel the desire from their kiss, the unusual undercurrent that made her body buzz, the still burned-on sensual taste of his lips on hers.

"Remember me?" a handsome, smartly dressed man asked. "I was a year ahead of you in high school."

Jenny explained, "Jesse recently bought the sporting goods store."

Celeste did remember Jesse, who'd been a football star in high school.

He had black curly hair, snapping dark brown eyes and a smile that could charm. "Which sport's your favorite?" he asked.

Clay stepped in, eyed Celeste's upswept hair, her dangling copper earrings, as well as the rest of her, in a millisecond glance. "Celeste prefers hiking. We were in the same club in high school and she can follow a trail better than anyone I know."

"Anyone but you," she acknowledged easily, wondering why he'd stepped in.

"You two were in the same class?" Jesse asked.

They glanced at each other and couldn't look away. The kiss was there in Clay's eyes—desire-filled, inciting, worrying.

Jesse cleared his throat, glanced at Clay, then asked

Celeste with a bit of challenge, "Can I get you a drink?" He motioned toward the wet bar. "Silas's bartender makes great dirty martinis."

"Thank you. Maybe in a little while. I need to talk to Clay about something."

"I'll find you in a little while," he agreed. He turned away and ambled over to the bar.

Clay led Celeste to a furniture grouping away from the others. "Lining up a date?" he asked in a serious tone.

"No, just trying not to be rude to one of Silas's guests. Do you have a problem with that?"

Consternation crossed Clay's face. "No, I guess not."

Celeste glanced around and made sure nobody was within earshot. "I need to tell you something about Abby. When we were together yesterday, we played with her dollhouse."

A smile crossed Clay's lips. "She likes to take everything out and then put it all back in again."

Celeste laughed. "Maybe she'll be an interior designer someday."

"But that's not what you wanted to tell me."

Her smile faded. "She played with a mom and dad and baby, but after a few minutes, she set the woman doll away from the dollhouse. When I asked her why, she said the mommy doll went away. I didn't know how you'd want me to deal with it."

Clay's smile slid away, and he shook his head. "My mother never said anything about the way Abby plays."

"Maybe your mom didn't notice, or maybe Abby felt free to do that with me since I haven't been part of her family circle."

Clay rammed his hands into the pockets of his khaki slacks. "I can't tell her Zoie's gone for good and I can't tell her she's coming back. You know Zoie's unpredictable, and I can't pin her down. When we divorced, sole custody was my main concern. In September, she'll be receiving the second half of her settlement. When we talk about where to wire it, we're going to have to get a few more things clarified. Abby needs to know who makes up her world."

Because Clay looked so troubled, Celeste regretted telling him about Abby's play. "I didn't mean to just throw this at you, but I thought you should know."

After a few moments of glancing away, his attention seemingly on the group across the room, he swung back to her. "What *did* you tell her?" His penetrating study of her face said he wanted the truth.

"I just suggested she let the daddy put the baby to bed, then we moved on to her pet-shop toys. I didn't want to make a big deal of it, and I certainly had no answers."

"I suppose I was naive to think she wouldn't remember Zoie leaving."

"Maybe. Or possibly, she's heard you and your mom talk. Mikala has often said kids are like sponges, soaking up words and feelings and vibrations that adults can't even intuit."

"You've talked to Mikala about this?" He didn't seem angry, just curious.

"No, but she and I had a few discussions before I decided to become a surrogate."

"I thought Zoie talked you into it."

She remembered how her sister had pleaded with her, the lists of reasons why Celeste should do this for all of them. She also remembered Clay's silence, his refusal to persuade her one way or the other. "I would do almost anything for my sister. But I had to make sure I was doing what I thought was right for all of us. The thing is, I didn't have all the facts then. You and Zoie kept her affair from me. I didn't know about that until she sent a long email, telling me the two of you were separating."

The sound of raucous laughter came from the group of men. One of the men had turned on a flat-screen TV in the corner to check sports scores. Jenny was helping Martha serve more hors d'oeuvres.

"I don't want to discuss this here," Clay said evenly.

Celeste had the feeling he didn't want to discuss it at all. "Your life with Zoie affected me, too, Clay, just as I'm affecting your life now. All of us made choices and some of them are mistakes."

"Do you believe being our surrogate was a mistake?"

"Not when I look at Abby," she said gently. "Not when I see how much you love her."

The conflict in Clay's eyes shifted to pain, and she wondered what he was thinking. But he'd never confide in her. After all, she'd made sure she'd never been close enough to him for confidences.

Glancing away from Clay assessing her and her motivation, she spotted Jesse watching her. She didn't want to seem rude, yet she wasn't interested in a date. She could sense his interest and knew that's where a conversation would be headed...unless she told him some facet of the truth.

"I don't know how to ask you this," she said, turning back to Clay.

"Just ask."

"When people want to know why I've come back to Miners Bluff and why I'm staying, I'd like to tell them the truth—that I'm here to get to know my daughter. Will that bother you?"

His mouth tightened into a straight line. "Maybe you

could hold off on any declarations of intent. We don't know where this is going."

"*I* do."

"Celeste," he said, with hoarse frustration. "You're pushing hard. Give me and Abby a chance to catch our breath."

Silas Decker's booming voice suddenly rang through the room. "Attention everyone. We're all going to settle into my home theater where we can watch my son's newest blockbuster. Martha will show you to the buffet and you can enjoy dinner while you watch."

"I guess Zack has a new movie," Celeste mused to break the tension between her and Clay.

"From what Silas has said, it could be another Oscar winner. Zack has definitely found his niche as a filmmaker. I'm probably going to cut out as soon as it's over," Clay said. "I know we still have a lot to discuss. Maybe we should do it on neutral ground."

"Such as?"

"My parents are taking Abby to a children's play in Flagstaff on Sunday afternoon. How would you like to go hiking with me on Moonshadow Mountain?"

Celeste's heart beat fast as she remembered the purple cliffs leading to the peak where the world seemed far away beneath.

"I promise we'll take it slow. You might not be used to the altitude yet."

His voice had a reassuring quality to it, but she didn't want reassurance.

What she wanted was to prove to him she was *not* her twin.

Chapter Four

Celeste's footsteps were muffled by the soft carpet of pine needles that cut through the forest. Ponderosas stood scattered between Douglas firs along a path that had been carved out decades ago and seemed to renew itself each year.

As she and Clay climbed out of the shadows into the sun, her boot hit a clump of earth, and stones clattered in the silence.

Clay turned quickly, ready to lunge to catch her just as he would any tourist he was guiding to the peak. When he saw she was still upright, he smiled and came to her side.

As he scrutinized her, she adjusted her backpack. "What?" she asked, feeling self-conscious.

"You haven't complained once and you've kept up the whole way."

"I haven't hiked a lot lately. But soon I'll be as familiar with this trail as I was when we were in high school."

Her open intention to stay unsettled him for a moment. But then he turned the conversation away from the present to the past. "You didn't have any restrictions when you were in high school, did you?"

Their mom had worked a lot, from noon to midnight most days. There had never been any discussion about curfews and rules. "I suppose not."

"Zoie never cared how late she was out. But you did. You seemed to have your own rules. Why was that?"

"You think I was too quiet to get into trouble?"

"Weren't you?"

"I didn't seek out trouble, if that's what you mean. I didn't go looking for the adrenaline rush. Even when I came up here, it was to find peace and some sense of myself, not to see how high I could climb or how near I could go to the edge of the cliff. That just wasn't me."

She knew what he was thinking. *That was Zoie.*

"But you're different now?"

"I do seek thrills once in a while," she joked, holding back a smile, not taking offense.

"Like " he prompted.

Thrills like falling in love with a pilot and getting her heart stomped on. "Going out on my own in business was an adventure for me. It was a risk, but I took it enthusiastically and didn't look back."

He took off his hat, folded it and stuck it in his waistband. "That wasn't the first thing that came into your mind, was it?"

"So now you're a psychic?"

"No, but your eyes give away more than you want them to."

Did they? Or was she subconsciously trying to send him some kind of message? "Maybe we should find a spot for lunch."

"Maybe you're trying to change the subject and avoiding talking about your romantic past," he returned quickly with an arched brow.

She ignored his attempt to probe. "There used to be a clearing over the next rise. It might be a good spot." It was just below Starfall Point, a guardrailed lookout over the town and valley below, where she and Zoie had often hiked as teenagers. She doubted if she and Clay would hike up there today. Something about Starfall Point was a little too intimate.

"Have it your way for now, but after we eat maybe you'll tell me what I want to know."

She was afraid to find out what that really was. Maybe today was like an interview, to see how fit she was to spend time with Abby. Today might have nothing to do with their kiss. She shouldn't be foolish enough to think there was more to it.

Pines and aspens gave way to a clearing where golden columbine attracted butterflies, where white yarrow seemed to blossom everywhere. This mountain haven hadn't changed much since she was a teenager. That was comforting in a world that seemed to be spinning under her feet.

Clay pulled a thin silver blanket from his backpack and shook it out under the aspens. Along with that he produced two baguettes, a hunk of cheese, beef jerky and two bottles of water. To their feast, Celeste added trail mix Mikala's aunt had made, along with two bunches of grapes and a ziplock bag of strawberries.

Clay leaned back on his palms and took a long breath of the fresh air. Celeste watched his face as he took in the view. She hadn't seen him relaxed since she'd arrived.

"Do you get much time to just do this, without bringing tourists along?"

He focused all of his attention on her. His navy T-shirt stretched across his chest. His biceps were defined, the muscles on his forearms obviously strong. Fishing, rafting and rock climbing were as much a part of his usual activities as driving his SUV to a vortex in Sedona or riding a mule down the Grand Canyon.

"I don't get out on my own as much as I'd like," he responded. "Not anymore. But I try to take a couple of days a month. Once in a while I go up to our cabin near the old mine."

"Is it still equipped?"

"With the woodstove and a lot of history. My great-grandfather built it because he had nowhere else to live. The woodstove is new for safety's sake and we keep a supply of bottled water up there. The root cellar still keeps supplies fresh. There's an old cot that's better than the floor, and with a sleeping bag it's comfortable. The cabin is a great escape. Once in a while, tourists who are brave enough to explore the area around the mine take a peek." He opened the bag with the cheese, offered it to her, then took a piece himself.

"The copper mine itself was boarded shut," Celeste mused, tearing off a piece of a baguette to have with the cheese. "But there are always some sightseers who want to see everything."

"We keep it stocked and unlocked. If anyone really needs to use it, well, that's why my great-grandfather built it."

"Do you ever take Abby along?"

The relaxed look fell away from Clay. He sat up, cross-legged and picked up a strip of beef jerky. "I haven't yet. We explore around the house when we go on walks."

"I'd bring her here," Celeste said, watching Clay as

he ate, remembering everything about their kiss. "It's a beautiful place. Abby could learn about the trees and the kinds of flowers that grow here. She might even see an elk or a rabbit or a ram if she's lucky."

"I don't want her to be frightened."

"If you're here to explain everything to her, she won't be frightened."

"She's already having bad dreams. I don't want to feed them."

"Clay, how can hiking up the mountain with her feed spooky dreams? This is beauty, sunshine and joy. I think Abby would love it."

"She's only three and a half. How old were you when you first came up here?"

"Believe it or not, my mother brought me and Zoie up here when we were about five. The history of Miners Bluff was her history, too. The Tin Pan Tavern, where she worked, had been around almost since the first claims were staked. But more than that, she needed an escape, too. She just warned us never to come up here alone."

"But you did."

"I first hiked up here alone when I was fourteen." Celeste remembered the day well. "Zoie had become a cheerleader and had a new group of friends. She wanted to include me but I could tell they didn't want me around. So she left school with them to go to the gym to practice and I headed up here."

"Were you scared?"

"I was defiant and I was determined to hike to Starfall Point on my own and get back before my mother missed me."

"Did you?"

"I did. That first hike taught me self-reliance. I learned

I could be a person on my own, outside of Zoie…that we didn't have to be interested in the same things."

"Had you been before then?"

"Before she became interested in cheerleading, we did everything together. Mom was always working and we took care of each other."

"You took care of Zoie, or Zoie took care of you?" he asked perceptively, cutting through any diplomatic answer she might give.

"I guess I took care of her and she entertained me. We were partners in growing up. I knew we had different talents. We banded together because Mom worked so much, because in our bedroom alone at night, we heard the sound of men's laughter underneath our feet and we were scared together." Now why had she told him that? Had Zoie ever discussed formative memories with him?

Clay forgot his food, interested in a way that told her this *was* the first he was hearing any of this. "Did anything ever happen to the two of you *because* of the bar?"

She and Zoie never talked about their childhoods, the way they lived, getting meals on their own when they were still young, pretty much taking care of themselves. She could just brush off Clay's question, but if she did, he'd probably know she wasn't being completely truthful.

So she answered, "Almost. Once. Mom was always super careful to keep the door locked that led up the stairway to our rooms. But our bedroom didn't have a lock. One night, I guess she didn't secure the downstairs door. A customer wandered up and came into our bedroom. Zoie screamed and I got the broom from the closet. I think he was as scared as we were. He ran out of there faster than he came in, practically falling down the stairs. Zoie and I went to the hardware store the next day and found a doorknob with a lock. Old Mr. Kenner told us exactly how to put it on and lent us the tools to do it. We paid for the lock out of our lunch fund."

"Lunch fund?"

"Zoie and I would often share one lunch so we could save the money from the second."

"Celeste!" His tone was aghast. "I knew you didn't live under the best of circumstances, but living like that—no child should live in fear or eat just half a lunch." Clay was quiet for a few moments. "Maybe that's why Zoie always wanted to go to such expensive restaurants."

"Trying to wipe away bad memories? It's possible. But Zoie likes to experience new and different things on a regular basis. You know that."

When she saw an angry look on his face, she quickly said, "Oh, Clay, I didn't mean—"

"Let's face it, Celeste. That's true. That's why she had the affair."

"I don't think she just wanted someone different." They had never talked about this.

"I don't want to get into it," Clay muttered.

Maybe they should. Maybe they had to.

Zoie and Clay had been a couple their senior year in high school. The four years Clay attended the University of Northern Arizona in Flagstaff, she'd waitressed at an upscale restaurant there. With a double major in finance and environmental sciences, Clay had often been closeted in the library or out on assignment, studying area specimens. With her own circle of friends, Zoie hadn't seemed to mind. Her letters had been full of social activities and plans for her engagement and marriage to Clay after he graduated. But then not long into their marriage, she'd complained to Celeste about Clay choosing to start a guiding service rather than staying in banking. Before their fifth anniversary, she'd had an affair, been in an accident on her way to meet her lover and had injuries so serious the surgeon had performed a partial hysterectomy. Celeste hadn't known until her sister left Clay that she'd been unfaithful and had used Celeste's surrogacy and Abby to try to hold her marriage together—a plan that had failed abysmally.

Celeste didn't feel she could push Clay on too many levels right now, not and manage visitation rights with Abby.

But she did need answers. "I need to know something, Clay."

"What is it?" He sat forward, watching her and listening.

She took a strawberry, popped it into her mouth, slowly chewed and swallowed, maybe trying to buy some time. When she glanced up at him again, his gaze was on her lips. She crooked her legs underneath her, but didn't lean any closer to him. He seemed to be dripping male energy today. He tangled her insides and sent shivers up her arms.

"When Zoie asked me to be her surrogate, was your marriage solid again?"

His lips tightened, and she could see the pulse beat at his temple. Then he said in a measured tone, "I thought we were on solid ground. We'd gone to counseling for a year before she asked you. After the divorce, I went over every one of those sessions and what she said, looking for hidden meanings. But the only thing I found was my inability to see through what she was doing."

"I don't understand."

"When Zoie decided she wanted something, she went

after it full throttle. After the accident and her partial hysterectomy, I'm not sure of the process that ticked through her head. I don't know if she felt she'd changed as a woman. I don't know what her motives were. But I know when we were in that counselor's office, she gave all the right answers. They seemed heartfelt at the time. Maybe she was lying to both of us. We had years invested in our marriage and I truly thought that was as important to her as it was to me. In that counselor's office, she made it seem as if it was. When we talked about having a child, I thought we were on solid ground again."

"I could feel Zoie's restlessness," Celeste told him. "I thought it was because she wanted to have a baby so badly. I should have known there was more to it. She's not the nurturing type."

"Are you?" he asked, reaching out and brushing a strand of hair the breeze had caught away from Celeste's cheek.

She could feel the calluses on the pads of his fingers and her whole body quivered. Somehow she found her voice. "I believe I am."

But was she nurturing enough? If she was, why had Peter had an affair with a flight attendant while he was in Italy? On top of that, why hadn't he used protection with his lover? Why had he so easily accepted responsibility for their unborn child and moved to Naples? Had he used her until the "right" woman came along?

"What are you thinking?" Clay prompted. "Your eyes went all dark like you were somewhere else."

"It doesn't matter. I'm here now."

Indeed she *was* here, so close to Clay again, she caught the hint of his soap. His eyes were locked to hers, as if he was attempting to see into her.

"That kiss of ours is haunting me," he admitted.

"I know. I mean, I've been thinking about it, too."

"I shouldn't even be considering kissing you again."

"Are you considering it?" The idea of heartache paled alongside the image of what could happen in Clay's arms.

He shook his head and then smiled. "Damn it, Celeste, this isn't you. This isn't like you at all, flirty and..."

"I'm *not* flirting with you!" She wasn't a tease and never had been. On the other hand, Clay was bringing out feelings she didn't know what to do with.

He leaned closer. "Then what do you call it when your eyes pull me closer, when you don't run or pull away?"

She didn't know why, but she blurted out, "You don't trust me."

"Should I?" he asked, even as he leaned in.

There had to be at least a thousand reasons for her to turn away or run or pull away, but as his lips touched hers, she couldn't think of one of them.

The kiss began slowly. Maybe Clay had decided just to taste a little pleasure and then back away, finish his lunch and leave unaffected. But that taste only whetted their appetites. That taste was a bell that couldn't be unrung. She was in his arms and he was in hers.

This moment was more important than any that had gone before. Clay had always been responsible and restrained. She'd never acted coy or flirted with him because she'd known he wasn't hers...would never be hers. But now with the world turned upside down and the future up for grabs, she decided to give in to everything she'd denied for so long.

Suddenly Clay pulled away, separating their bodies as if she was too hot to touch and he was getting burned.

They sat under the shade of the aspen, breathing fast

and hard, letting their emotions and their body rhythms return to normal. Except *what* was normal?

"Was I a substitute this time?" she asked softly, her voice shaky even in her attempt to steady it.

He turned to face her. "No." His level voice held truth.

Still, she thought, he could *believe* that was the truth. Yet was it? She was Zoie's twin. He'd never shown any interest in her before. Not that she'd wanted him to. She'd never want a man who could look at another woman while being involved with someone. Yet Peter had been that type of man and she hadn't known it. She hadn't even guessed. She'd been so stupid! Yet she hadn't known Peter all her life. She *had* known Clay.

"Rebound" was a word she had to consider carefully along with another—"revenge."

Was Clay so bitter and resentful of Zoie that he would take it out on her? That he would use her until he no longer wanted her?

Then what would happen to Abby?

"What are we doing, Clay? I'm sitting here wondering about your motives and you're probably wondering about mine."

"Twice. I gave in to lust twice. That's not like me, Celeste. I've been a damn monk since before Zoie and I split. Then I feel this attraction to you… Everything's under control and then…we explode."

He sent her a wry look. "Unless it's not like that for you. Maybe I just imagined all that heat because I haven't felt anything like it for so long."

"You didn't imagine it," she said softly. "But what are we going to do about it?"

He opened a bottle of water and drank half of it, then

he set it down with a thump. "We're going to ignore it and pretend it doesn't exist."

Pretend it didn't exist? She knew her desire for Clay was based on more than lust. But on his side...even if this had nothing to do with Zoie, she'd simply been an available pretty woman and he'd responded as most men would.

"I think we should keep limiting our time together," he went on. "When you see Abby, I'll make sure I'm not there."

On one hand, she was thrilled he wasn't keeping her from Abby. But on the other, she suspected if they ignored what was happening between them, it wouldn't go away on its own.

Not if it had any basis at all.

Celeste dove into the everyday work, play and distractions of Miners Bluff in between her visits with Abby. For the past two weeks, she'd learned some of her daughter's likes and dislikes and grown to appreciate her sweet nature. But she hadn't seen Clay during her visits...and she really missed him.

So today she'd volunteered to help Mikala at the annual Historic Homes Arts Fair. It promoted tourism and funded the constant renovation costs of old buildings. Paintings hung on pegboards. Jewelry crafters laid out sterling and semiprecious stones atop velvet cloths. Ceramic pots of all shapes, sizes and colors abounded as did knitted and crocheted shawls and sweaters, wood-crafted items and whirligigs for front yards. Celeste was helping Mikala focus on children's creativity. Under a tent in the town park, her students gave impromptu concerts on violins, keyboards and flutes.

Miners Bluff was laid out like a wagon wheel. The

park was the center, a circle of green lawn with trees and benches and a large gazebo. A sign at each of its entrances gave a summary of the town's history. The children's music tent was located near a few live oaks that cast shade over it in the early afternoon. Three of Mikala's students had just finished Beethoven's Moonlight Sonata.

Suddenly Celeste was almost knocked over by a child gripping her around the legs. Balancing herself and stooping down, she saw Abby gazing up at her.

"C'leste! C'leste! Gran-daddee's gonna buy me a snow cone."

Celeste hugged Abby and brushed her bangs across her forehead. "He is? What flavor is your favorite?"

She cast a glance at Clay's father standing only about a foot away. He was almost as tall as Clay, his dark brown hair streaked with gray over the temples, his black-framed glasses sitting high on his nose. He'd gained weight over the past few years, but his khaki slacks and oxford shirt still fit impeccably. He hadn't seemed to have lost even an ounce of his starch.

"Owange," Abby pronounced proudly. "That's my fav'ite.

"There's Daddy," Abby said, spinning around and running toward her father who was making his way toward them.

This was the first time Celeste had come face-to-face with the elder Sullivan since she'd returned. "Hello, Mr. Sullivan."

"Celeste," he said stiffly with a slight tilt to his head. "I hear you're back in town to get to know Abby."

Glancing toward Clay, Celeste noticed he'd picked up his daughter. She was babbling away as she pointed toward Celeste. Clay's gaze met hers and the air seemed to shiver between them.

As if Harold Sullivan felt it, too, he frowned. "You can't confuse her."

"I don't intend to confuse her."

"You look like her mother."

"That's beyond my control. Zoie's not in her life and might not be again."

"You want her to call you *Mom?*"

The man was not going to make her back down even though he'd always seemed to think he had more clout than anyone else in Miners Bluff. "I can only dream of that happening someday. For now, I just want to be around as a guiding force."

"Guiding her toward *what* is the question."

As Clay and Abby approached them, Mr. Sullivan lowered his voice. "I have to wonder if you're here for other reasons than Abby."

Celeste felt her back stiffen in reaction. "What reasons would those be?"

"Maybe like your sister, you want a nice settlement, another piece of Clay's trust fund. Or maybe unlike Zoie, you have the fortitude to stick around until you could inherit all of it."

Although she was shocked by the accusations, she wouldn't let Mr. Sullivan see that. His attitude towards Clay's aspirations in life had always colored her view of him. Was he really as intolerant as he seemed? If he was a loving father, wouldn't he want Clay to be happy? But now she could see Mr. Sullivan wanted what *he* wanted, and what anyone else thought or cared simply didn't matter. Arguing with him about her intentions would have no value to this banker.

Clay and Abby were beside them then, and Abby

practically jumped out of Clay's arms reaching for Celeste.

"You might be too heavy..." Clay began.

But Celeste shook her head, taking her daughter into her arms. "She's fine." Her hands were shaking a bit from her exchange with his father, but holding Abby covered that.

Abby was pointing to a little girl with a flute. "I wanna play it."

"Maybe you can when you're a little older." Clay's arm brushed Celeste's as he turned to look at the children. They both stopped, immobilized for a moment.

Harold said gruffly, "I'm going to go get that snow cone. Why don't I meet you over at O'Rourke's stand?"

Clay's gaze went to his daughter, who seemed to be mesmerized by the instruments. "We could be here a little while. Why don't you just come back here?"

"If you say so." His father headed off toward a vending cart.

"Down, down, down," Abby demanded.

"You can't go very far," Celeste told her. "You might get lost in all these people."

Mikala, who had been supervising the children, took Abby's hand. "Do you want to come over here with me and look at the keyboard?"

Abby raised her gaze to Clay, and he gave her a nod.

When she had joined the child of about twelve, who was standing at the keyboard, Clay moved closer to Celeste and asked in a private tone, "What did my father say to you?"

"How do you know he said anything?" She wasn't sure whether she should cover for Harold Sullivan or make more waves between him and his son.

"You were delighted to see Abby and all of a sudden

you went pale. He's tried to interfere in my life enough over the years. I want to know what he said."

"He's tried to interfere in something other than your line of work?"

"Don't change the subject."

She gave a small sigh, knowing it would be best to be completely straight up with Clay. "He implied I'm here for other reasons than to get to know Abby."

"Other reasons?"

Clay's lips were close to her ear so she could hear him above the chatter and noise of the throng around them. His breath on her cheek and her body's response to it made her wonder if old longings had urged her back to Miners Bluff, too.

But for now, she answered, "Money. He thinks I'm here for your money, if not one way, then another."

When Clay shook his head and stepped back, Celeste saw the lines of resolve furrow his brow. She pleaded, "Don't say anything to him, Clay. I doubt if he'll listen to you."

"You're definitely right about that."

"He might think he's protecting Abby by trying to chase me away."

"*Can* he chase you away?" Clay's tone had that resolute get-to-the-bottom-of-it quality again that had become such a part of him since his divorce.

"No, he can't," Celeste answered, making her tone as determined as she knew how.

But then she caught sight of Harold Sullivan approaching them once more, an orange snow cone in his hand. Clay stepped closer to her again, as if he meant to protect her from this father.

When she gazed up at him, neither seemed to be able

to look away. But then Clay broke eye contact and she knew he was rejecting the bond she felt between them.

What good was that bond if only *she* could embrace it?

Chapter Five

Clay knocked on the door of Celeste's suite at the Purple Pansy. He hadn't seen her for almost three weeks... on purpose. He knew how she was interacting with his daughter. His mother always gave him a full report. She even snapped pictures now and then. And when he looked at them, when Celeste appeared in erotic dreams he tried to banish from his mind, he wanted to see her and kiss her again.

But he wasn't here tonight because he was drawn to her. He was here because she was starting something he had to stop.

When she opened the door, his words seemed to vanish. In a pink top and jeans, her hair tied up in a ponytail, she made him feel they were both fifteen years younger again. But they weren't, and he had to deal with what was happening now.

"Clay," she said with a surprised smile. Then the smile faded. "Is Abby okay?"

"She's fine. I need to talk to you about something. Can I come in?"

Looking puzzled, she backed away from the door and invited him into the sitting area. It was two rooms, really. He could see she'd been working at the library table against the inside wall. A laptop was front and center as well as a printer. Papers were strewn here and there. Mikala's aunt had decorated the room in flowers and stripes, yellow-and-blue with earth tones thrown in. He could see through the arched doorway into the bedroom beyond. But his gaze didn't linger there...wouldn't linger there.

"Did I interrupt your work?" He gestured toward the computer.

"That's okay. I was going to break to get something for supper."

"At a restaurant?" Suddenly the idea of sitting on the sofa with Celeste to talk about anything didn't seem like a very wise thing to do.

"No. Anna makes casseroles every day so I can share if I want. Tonight Mikala has music lessons all evening in her studio and Anna had a meeting with the Preservation Society to talk about that new museum the Chamber wants to build. Would you like to share the casserole? I can heat it up."

Anna's kitchen sounded like a much better idea than Celeste's private quarters. And he *hadn't* eaten. Maybe what he wanted to say to Celeste would go down better in the friendly atmosphere of Anna's kitchen. He'd spent time there as a teenager with Mikala, Zoie and Celeste, Jenny, Dawson and Zack. They'd all known Anna's biscotti jar was always filled, just as her fridge was always stocked with chocolate milk.

"Let me get some shoes," Celeste said, going into the bedroom for her sneakers.

Clay didn't move. He wasn't going anywhere near that bedroom. He wasn't getting too close to Celeste. Their kisses had rocked him more than he wanted to admit. Attraction to Celeste was taboo on *so* many levels.

"Your mom said you had an overnight trip last week," she called from the bedroom.

"I did," he called back. "Campers who wanted to spend a night or two at Oak Creek."

In spite of trying to avoid glancing that way, he could see Celeste perched on the edge of a green-and-tan flowered chair. She crossed her left leg over her right and bent to tie her shoe. Her legs were long and lithe. She was an inch taller than Zoie. It didn't seem like much, but it gave her a willowyness that Zoie didn't possess. She uncrossed her legs and bent to tie her right shoe.

Looking up at him, she asked, "Did they have a good time?"

Watching her hands, her silky ponytail bobbing with her movement, he'd almost forgotten what they were talking about. "I hope they did. They said they're going to come back to the area again next year and want me to take them down the Grand Canyon."

Celeste rose to her feet and came toward him. "I haven't done that since I was back here for vacation when I was nineteen. I wouldn't mind doing it again sometime, maybe even white-water rafting."

He wasn't going to offer to take her, not after what had happened on their hiking trip.

"All ready," she said and went to the door.

He reached around her and opened it. Zoie would have spent a half hour in the bathroom with her makeup products before she was ready to go even to the kitchen.

But as he caught the scent of Celeste's honeysuckle lotion or shampoo or whatever it was, he began to realize what Celeste had been trying so hard to tell him. She *wasn't* Zoie. She was really trying to act like a mother to his daughter. She certainly seemed genuine. But he'd been fooled before.

Ignoring the tilt of her smile, the precious-gem green of her eyes, the silky golden long strands in her light brown hair, he motioned for her to precede him down the hall to the house's main kitchen.

Celeste's guest suite was on the first floor. Mikala and her aunt's sleeping quarters were on the second, and the largest guest suite complete with a small kitchen was on the third. The whole place seemed to have the light scent of vanilla and lavender. The house, which was about a hundred years old, was well maintained yet quaintly old-fashioned with bronze sconces that looked like oil lamps, ceiling lighting with chandelier bulbs and wallpaper with tiny flowers. Anna's sense of caring seemed to permeate it all. He supposed that's why he, like some of his classmates, had been drawn here as teenagers. Even now, the house seemed as welcoming as his own.

"Are you comfortable here?" he asked Celeste, wondering if she felt the same way.

"Oh, yes. Absolutely. In fact, I almost feel too comfortable. I've been here over a month. Mikala is right upstairs. Her aunt is always ready with a story to tell or a glass of tea to share. Remember the gallons of chocolate milk we drank here?"

As she said it, they entered the kitchen, and he stopped abruptly. "What happened here? I can see my reflection in every appliance."

Celeste laughed. "I think Anna's refrigerator lasted a long time, but it was born before we were. The rest of the appliances went down the same path, so Mikala convinced her to update, at least that part of the kitchen, and the counters and the floor. But other than that—"

He had to chuckle. He did recognize the mahogany clock that still hung above the sink, the railing above the cupboards holding Hummel figurines, the maple table and chairs, antiques still polished and suiting this kitchen perfectly.

"She had to make new purple pansy curtains," Celeste said, going to the refrigerator. "But they're the same café style that I remember from years ago." She took out a casserole and removed the lid. "It looks like pasta and beef. How does that sound?"

"Anything I don't have to cook sounds wonderful. Here, let me get that." The casserole looked heavy and he'd stepped in automatically to take it and put it in the microwave, but Celeste didn't protest.

Rather, she simply set the timer and said, "I'll toss the salad, and if we're still hungry when we're finished—" She pointed to the dessert holder on the counter. "She baked a peach pie this morning. I'm definitely going to gain weight if I stay here too much longer."

"*Much longer* meaning…?" he prompted.

She took carrots, lettuce and celery from the fridge and straightened. "I'm going to have to start looking for an apartment. I don't need much room, but I'd like a first floor with a backyard where Abby can play."

Clay felt a stab of panic. Could he ever let his daughter stay with Celeste? Even to let her babysit? Could he trust her? If she wanted her daughter badly, what would she be willing to do? Run with Abby in her arms?

"What are you thinking?" Celeste asked, maybe as aware of him as he was of her.

Nothing that I want you to know, he thought, staying silent.

"Clay, what?"

"You seem to think it might be easy for me to just let Abby come see you wherever you are."

Celeste turned toward him, reached a hand out to him, then seemed to think better of it and let it drop to her side. "No, I don't think it would be easy. Yet if you become comfortable enough with the idea, it doesn't have to be hard. Unless…" Her gaze seemed to study every detail on his face, from the lines he knew were creasing his forehead to the stubble of beard on his chin.

"She'd be safe with me, Clay. I know about choking hazards and cleaning supplies kids shouldn't get into. I'm not irresponsible."

"I don't know that, do I?"

"You could soon figure it out if you were around when I visited Abby."

"You and I both know it's better if I'm not."

Her face took on some color. She turned back to the greens she'd pulled from the refrigerator, snagged a bowl from the cupboard and began tearing lettuce.

Suddenly she stopped. "It's more than that, isn't it? You think I might try to take her from you."

"I never said that."

"No, but it ran through your head."

Their gazes locked and he couldn't deny it. If he was reading her right, that thought actually hurt her.

The microwave beeped, and he knew this preliminary conversation was going to make the reason he came here tonight even more difficult to talk about.

They finished making preparations for supper. He stirred the casserole, covered it and reinserted it in the microwave for another minute. Celeste put the salad together and set it on the table. She placed dishes on the purple pansy place mats with silverware and napkins beside them.

Finally, after they were seated, water poured, and a few bites taken, Celeste asked, "Why did you come tonight, Clay? If you don't want to be around when I see Abby, you certainly don't want to be alone with me."

He took a couple of bites trying to figure out the best way to say what he had to say. "You've been giving Abby presents."

Celeste's eyes widened. "Is there something wrong with the doll I gave her? It was soft with no small parts and could be washed."

"There's nothing wrong with it. She sleeps with it and carries it around with her."

"That's the problem? She prefers it to her other toys?"

"No. Lord, Celeste, how petty do you think I am?"

Celeste's eyes took on a defiant glint. "I don't know. Because you're not really telling me what's bothering you. Yesterday when I brought over the sweater set, your mom said it was just the right size."

"It was. It was as perfect as the little bows you bought for her hair, the board puzzles, the toy with flashing lights to teach her colors. You're trying to buy your way into her affections and that has to *stop*."

Celeste's fork stopped midway from her plate to her mouth. She stared at him as if he had two heads, as if she were going to deny what he had said.

More gently now, he added, "If you want to visit and play with her, that's fine. But don't lead her to think every time she sees you, you're going to give her another present. That's not fair to her or to you."

An expression crossed Celeste's face that worried Clay.

Had he said too much? Should he have even brought this up?

Before he could answer his own questions, she'd put down her fork, risen to her feet and stepped over to the counter where she made some noises with the coffeepot. He could tell she wasn't interested in coffee. Whatever was troubling her, he gave in to the urge to find out what it was. After all, it could affect his daughter.

Forgetting his own dinner, he pushed his chair back, purposely scraping the floor so she'd know he was getting up. Then he went to the counter and stood beside her as she tried to put a filter in the basket. He saw her face had paled, and now he was really worried. He clasped her shoulder, intending it just to be a measure of comfort. Instead, *he* reacted to the feel of her warmth under his hand. He didn't remove it.

"What's going on, Celeste?"

She shook her head and fumbled with the carafe, averting her face from his.

His thumb under her chin, he nudged her around until she faced him. Her eyes were bright with unshed tears. "I can't believe I'm doing what—" She shook her head again.

"I don't understand."

She took a couple of breaths and then tried again. "You know my mother had men friends, guys she'd bring up to the apartment after the bar closed."

"There was lots of gossip," he admitted. Especially after he'd started dating Zoie, his parents had discussed it more than once.

"A couple of the men stayed awhile. It wasn't just one night. I'd really forgotten all about this."

"Forgotten what?" Clay prompted gently.

"One of the men, his name was Derrick, was a really

nice guy. He didn't come up just after the bar closed. He was there for dinner for several months. On Sundays when he'd come for a meal, he'd bring Zoie and me presents—a new CD, baseball caps, a bracelet from the discount store. I don't know about Zoie, but I felt if he gave me a present, he must like me separate from Mom. I started dreaming about having a real family, two parents, a dad who worked, too, so Mom wouldn't have to work so hard."

"He didn't stay?"

"I don't know what happened. He and Mom started fighting, arguing, then he just stopped coming. No goodbye. No explanation. When I asked Mom about it, she got this strange look on her face. She just said, 'He had to move on' and she couldn't go with him. She had us to think about and a decent job and she couldn't take the chance a man would do what he said he was going to do."

Clay realized now that Celeste's mom had modeled behavior that Zoie and Celeste had reacted to very differently, though he hadn't known it. Zoie had wanted a partner to have fun with and to see the world with. And Celeste...it seemed she'd only wanted a family.

"I can't believe I was doing the same thing he did!" Celeste confessed with regret. "I can't believe I thought presents would make up for the years I didn't spend with her."

Stepping a little closer, Clay couldn't help himself from taking Celeste's face between his hands. "So now you realize that. It's okay, Celeste. No harm done."

Yet, he realized, lots of harm *had* been done. Celeste's childhood had impacted her. That impact had affected his marriage to Zoie, too. And now? Now he had to keep their kisses from impacting what happened next. He was so close to her. Her eyes were so bright and her expression so vulnerable.

Because of that, he dropped his hands and stepped away. He asked, "Do you really want coffee?"

She gave him a tremulous smile and answered, "I prefer tea. But I'll make you a pot if you'd like."

"No. I have to get going."

Understanding shone in her eyes. Understanding of why he'd backed away and why he was going to leave now...before the kiss began...before they did more.

After all, he was her sister's ex-husband. And he didn't trust women any more than she trusted men.

At a children's clothing shop, Celeste chose a pink T-shirt with a kitten appliquéd on the front and handed it to Clay. "Do you think Abby would like this?"

Clay had called her yesterday to invite her along to Flagstaff to shop for Abby's clothes and supplies for preschool.

He took the T-shirt in his large tanned hand, and Celeste remembered all too well the feel of that hand on her arms...at the back of her neck when he'd kissed her. She had to remain calm, cool and collected this afternoon. Ever since he'd picked her up—they'd already shopped at a few stores—she'd sensed he was on edge.

Because kissing was out of the question? Because she reminded him too much of Zoie? Because she wanted to intrude into Abby's life?

Any or all of the above.

He laid the shirt on the growing pile in the shopping basket he was carrying. "You do a good job of focusing in on the things she'll like." He paused, shuffling through the clothes in the basket. Then he met her gaze again. "I asked you along today because I thought it would be a good idea if we did something for her together. Do you know what I mean?" He was making it clear they had a purpose here today. It wasn't a date by any means. And she understood.

"She's easy to read, Clay, open and guileless and totally adorable. You've done a great job."

"Then why do I feel as if I'm letting her down? As if Zoie walking out was somehow my fault, and someday Abby will blame me for it?"

Did Clay realize what part he'd played in Zoie's desertion? Not that there were any excuses for a mother walking out on her child. Not that there were any excuses for a mother leaving and not coming back.

Did Zoie care about Abby now? How could she not? Celeste wasn't sure if she knew her sister anymore.

"As long as you give Abby all the love and attention she could ever want, as long as you give her boundaries, she'll know you were the parent who loved her."

"How do *you* know so much about kids?" he asked with a wry smile.

"I don't know so much about them. I just remember what being one felt like."

"Because you never knew who your father was?"

"That, and because Zoie and I spent a lot of time in that apartment alone."

Suddenly Clay's cell phone buzzed. He checked the screen. "It's Mom. I'd better take this."

Celeste didn't want to eavesdrop, but when she heard Clay ask, "Do you think she has a fever, too?" she moved a few steps closer.

"We'll be there as soon as we can. If possible, push liquids."

When he glanced at Celeste, she suspected his mother had asked something about her. He didn't hesitate when he said, "Yes, I'll be bringing her along with me. A half hour at the most."

Clay secured his phone on his belt. Before she could ask, he said, "Abby didn't want her usual snack. She said her stomach hurt. Shortly after, she started sneezing. Mom thinks she might have a fever but she doesn't have a thermometer there."

Celeste returned the T-shirt to the shelf. The expression on Clay's face told her he was more than a little worried about Abby's condition. "It's probably just a cold," he said.

"I'm sure you're right," Celeste agreed, reaching out and touching Clay's hand.

For a moment, true understanding flowed between them. But he didn't let the moment last long. He removed his hand and she dropped hers. They headed for the door, ready to race back to Miners Bluff and figure out exactly what was going on with their daughter.

The Sullivan home was located in one of Miners Bluff's older neighborhoods. A grand, two-story Colonial, the brick exterior had been refaced several times over the years. The huge front porch with black trim and white pillars was more for decoration than function.

Clay opened the door, Celeste right behind him as they entered a high-ceilinged foyer with a winding staircase that led to the second floor. Everywhere there was polished dark wood, crown molding, and a sense of the history that had begun in Miners Bluff with the Sullivans. Photos of the first copper mine hung above the credenza, where a finely carved replica of a wooden stagecoach stood.

The accoutrements didn't interest her as they passed through the living room, a grand dining room, to an oversized kitchen beyond. Granite counters and mahogany cupboards along with a Sub-Zero refrigerator spoke of a makeover here, too.

Beyond the kitchen there was a hall with another stairway. Clay went there and called upstairs. "Mom? Are you up there with Abby?"

Celeste heard Violet call back. "Yes, we are—in the guest room."

He took the steps two at a time, and Celeste hurried to keep up.

When they entered the pretty green bedroom, Celeste wondered if it had been refinished and redecorated for Abby. There was a white double bed trimmed in yellow and the other furniture matched. Abby was on the bed, a light throw tossed over her, while Violet sat on a chair beside the bed, a book on her lap. To Celeste's surprise, Clay's father also stood in the room, seemingly without purpose. His father's presence seemed to immobilize Clay for a moment. He nodded to his father, gave his mom's shoulder a squeeze and sat on the bed at Abby's feet.

But as soon as Abby saw him, she tossed off the cover and crawled straight into his arms. She sneezed twice, and he handed her a tissue from the box on the night stand.

"Grandma tells me you don't feel well."

"My tummy hurts and..." She started coughing.

Clay laid his hand on her back as if that would support her and give her comfort. "I brought someone else who was worried about you."

Abby looked up and saw Celeste. Where she'd been frowning before, now she gave more than half a smile. "C'leste." She reached up to her.

Celeste embraced the little girl. These hugs were

beginning to feel more real, more as if they mattered, more as if she might earn the right to have one on a daily basis. She sat on the bed holding Abby with Clay beside her, glancing at him to see if he thought this was okay.

The nerve in his jaw jumped, and he looked tense all over. Yet he didn't tell her to put Abby down. The child clung to her for a few minutes and then settled into her lap, as if it were the most natural thing in the world. Abby nestled her head against Celeste's breast, curled into her body and closed her eyes.

"I've been trying to coax her to sleep for the past hour. I didn't really want to call you, Clay, and interrupt."

"You didn't interrupt. We were almost finished." He brushed his hand up and down his daughter's arm. "I think you're going to like the clothes, especially the ones Celeste picked out. They definitely have a princess theme."

"I like the pwincesses," she said with her eyes still closed. "Awiel and Belle and Cind-a-wella," she murmured.

"And Snow White and Sleeping Beauty?" Celeste suggested.

Abby's eyes popped open. "Do you like them, too?"

"I sure do."

"Isn't that a nice coincidence?" Mr. Sullivan mumbled.

"Harold, Celeste is trying to make Abby feel better," his wife scolded.

"Maybe the best way to do that is to tuck her into bed and give her some soup. Or better yet, I can call Doc Wakemore," Harold said.

"I'll call Adam Cooper in the morning," Clay informed his dad. "He's her pediatrician. He'll know what's best."

"He just set up his practice in Miners Bluff. What does he know about anything yet?"

"He did a fellowship in Chicago. He also did some volunteer pediatric service in Haiti. He's more than well aware of what kids can contract. If Abby gets worse tonight, I'll call him. But if she doesn't, I'll wait till morning." He reached for his daughter then, but she tightened her arms around Celeste's neck.

"Stay wif C'leste," she mumbled.

"Do you mind?" he asked.

"Of course she doesn't mind," Harold interjected. "She can't wait to insinuate herself into your life, just like Zoie. Don't make this so easy for her."

Clay turned to face his father, anger etched on his face. "Dad, stop it. If you want to have a conversation about this, we'll have it alone, some other time. Not now."

"That's exactly how you got tied up with Zoie for almost a decade. You wouldn't have the conversation *now*. You wouldn't give up. You had to prove something to yourself and everybody who knew she'd had an affair. Look what that got you."

Violet had stood and gone to her husband's side. She tugged on his elbow. He glanced down at her and then sighed, "All right. Take Abby home. Just don't forget whose daughter she is."

Celeste heard the resentment and bitterness in Harold Sullivan's voice when he spoke of her sister and the marriage that had gone south. But she also sensed hostility between him and Clay. Like Silas and Zack Decker, Harold and Clay couldn't seem to find common ground, couldn't seem to get over expectations in order to have a relationship founded on who they actually were.

As she descended the steps with Abby, Clay watching

over her, she had no delusion that he'd forget even for a minute who was the parent here.

But maybe soon, she could convince him *she* knew how to be a parent, too. Maybe soon he'd realize she wanted to be part of his life as well as Abby's.

Chapter Six

Celeste sat right beside Abby's car seat, her arm draped around her protectively as Clay drove. There was a glassiness in Abby's eyes that scared her. She wished she could take in Abby's cold or flu so her daughter didn't have to suffer it.

Her daughter. She felt closer to her with each day.

Clay watched them in the rearview mirror. The worry in his eyes was clear. At a red light, he cast another glance over his shoulder at the backseat just as Celeste leaned close to Abby and put her hand on her chest. She closed her eyes, then opened them, staring directly into his.

"What?" he asked.

"She's getting more congested. I don't like it, Clay." Her voice was tremulous with emotion she'd never felt before. So this was what it was like to be a real mom.

"How can you tell?" The light turned green, and he

shifted his attention back to the traffic that was heavier than usual with end-of-August tourists.

"She's wheezing. She has a fever."

The only sound on the rest of the drive home was that of Abby's cough and her sniffles. Celeste held the little girl's hand, feeling absolutely helpless and hating it. She'd experienced it once before when she'd given Abby to Clay and Zoie.

Five minutes later, Clay parked in his garage and carried Abby into her room, laying her gently on the bed.

Clay ran his hand through Abby's hair, feeling her cheek. "She *is* warm. I'll get the thermometer."

In the meantime, Celeste asked Abby, "What would you like to do? We could read or watch a movie." She'd seen the stack of children's DVDs on the entertainment center in the great room.

"Watch a movie. Cind-a-wella Bawbie," Abby said decisively but then began coughing again.

With a worried frown, Clay returned with the temporal thermometer and directed the probe to Abby's forehead. "Stay still for a sec," he warned with a smile.

"I will," Abby murmured.

Clay slid the probe to her temple, then studied the reading. "Ninety-nine point nine. This could be just a cold." He sounded relieved at that idea and Celeste wondered if *she* could be overreacting.

"Why don't I get you something to drink while you get set up with a movie? How about apple juice?"

Abby nodded.

Celeste's gaze met Clay's. He couldn't hide his concern for his daughter, but he apparently knew what to do in this situation. Along with that concern, Celeste thought he was looking at *her* differently. With less cynicism?

She was afraid if she made a misstep, he'd throw her out of his life...out of Abby's life.

He was assessing her again when he said, "I can give you the keys to the SUV if you want to go back to Mikala's. I have a truck if I need to take Abby to the urgent care center."

Celeste went very still, unsure if he was giving her an opening to stay as well as go. "Do you want me to leave?"

"I don't think Abby's going to want to play tonight or look at the clothes and supplies we bought her."

Celeste's intuition told her Clay expected her to leave, not share responsibility for Abby. She could see defensiveness as well as determination in his stance. "No, of course she won't want to play. But I could make us all something to eat while you spend time with her. I want to help out, Clay. I don't have to be an invited guest."

Abby coughed again.

His focus on his daughter, Clay raked his fingers through his hair. "I'm going to set up the vaporizer. I think, ladybug, you can watch a movie on your portable DVD in *here*. Is that okay?"

Abby looked as if she were too tired to argue. She agreed with a condition. "You stay."

Unable to refuse her request, Clay sat on the bed beside Abby and looked at Celeste. "It would be a help if you could make us something to eat. The freezer's stocked with all kinds of stuff and so is the pantry."

"I'll see what I can find."

The electricity between her and Clay was still there, still swarming around them in spite of the circumstances. But they were both attempting to deny it. Just how long could they do that? What would happen when they got within touching distance again? What would happen if she let him kiss her and didn't stop whatever happened next?

"Thanks," he said, and she could see he meant it.

For the next hour, Celeste kept her mind focused on Abby and the food she was going to make for all of them. She knew Abby needed liquids. Finding chicken breasts in the freezer, she defrosted them in the microwave and used one to make broth while she used the rest to make a casserole along with some fresh broccoli. Pulling a can of soup from the pantry, Celeste mixed it with cream cheese and a few spices, concocting a sauce.

Soon the soup broth was steaming with carrots and celery. She'd add alphabet pasta for Abby when it was almost done. After topping the casserole with bread crumbs, she popped it in the oven.

With everything under control in the kitchen, she ventured into Abby's room with a glass of water garnished with a slice of lime. That might entice her to drink.

When Clay spied her in the doorway, he smiled. "Whatever you're making smells great."

"Thanks, I hope you like it. It should be finished in about forty-five minutes."

Clay lounged beside Abby on the bed, his long legs stretched out in front of him. He'd taken off his boots and pulled his shirt from his jeans. His stocking feet and the stubble on his chin made him look sexier than ever.

Propping himself on an elbow, he looked over at Abby. "She doesn't seem to be coughing as much."

"The vaporizer might be helping."

"I smoothed VapoRub on her throat, too."

Abby wrinkled her nose, showing she was listening to the conversation. "That stuff smells *awful*."

"But it's helping you breathe, isn't it?"

Abby swiveled her gaze from the DVD player to stare at Celeste. "Can you wcad to me?"

"I'm sure your dad would be glad to—"

"I want *you*. You wead diffewent."

"Different?" She knew children spoke in a language of their own. Different could possibly mean many things.

"Yeah. You wead like a girl. Daddy weads like a boy. When you wead a girl stowy, I like it better."

Celeste laughed. "I see. So you'd rather I read Cinderella but your dad can read Sponge Bob."

Abby smiled and gave a vigorous nod. Then she pounded on the bed. "Come here, too. You can sit. Daddy can listen."

Getting into the same bed with Clay, even under these circumstances, gave her goose bumps. "I might have to check on supper."

"That's okay. Wight, Daddy?"

"Sure. We can stop and go back to Cinderella Barbie while you do."

His voice was mock enthusiastic so she warned him, "Just wait until she wants you to help her decide which shoes to wear."

"She's only three and a half."

"Today she's three and a half. But these years are going to go so fast, you won't know what hit you."

"Neither will you." The tone of his voice wasn't challenging. It wasn't offensive. It was almost accepting.

The bed was a queen-size with a pink eyelet spread, so when Celeste got in to lie down next to Abby she almost felt—with the canopy above them—as if they were in a world of their own with Abby snuggled between them. They weren't touching, but facing each other, Celeste's knees bent toward Abby. Their feet weren't that far apart.

Celeste asked, "What would you like me to read?"

"The kitty book," Abby responded.

Celeste had read *Kitten's First Full Moon* to Abby once before. It was one of her favorites, she knew. She was beginning to learn a lot of things about her daughter, and she loved knowing her favorite things. Maybe that's why her own mom had sung her that song. Maybe that's why she'd remembered it.

Abby asked her dad, "Can I have Lulu?"

Lulu was propped down at the end of the bed against the footboard. Clay slung his foot down, caught the cat and brought it up within arm's reach. Then he wiggled it and walked it to Abby. "Lulu's ready to listen, too."

Abby wrapped her arm around the cat's middle and brought it in close.

A few minutes later, Celeste was reading, all the while aware of Abby listening and Clay watching. This enforced closeness with him on a bed, of all places, was awkward. Yet there was something more, too. Maybe the question of what would happen if they ever did share a bed bounced in their heads. Maybe the question of what would happen if Clay ever thought of Abby as her daughter nudged them both. The waters were so murky. Her attraction to Clay made her relationship with Abby more complicated. Yet her relationship with Abby gave her attraction to Clay even more meaning.

After Celeste finished reading, Clay opened the DVD player again, and she went to check on supper. She let Abby's soup cool a bit, then fixed plates for her and Clay. When she carried the dinner tray to the bedroom, Clay was still watching the movie with Abby.

He sat up when he saw her. "You don't have to serve us."

"I'm not serving exactly. I just thought we could have

a picnic in here—a picnic with soup and plenty of apple juice and more water. What do you think, Abby?"

"I'm not hungwy," she said with little energy.

Celeste didn't like the paleness of her cheeks, or the lack of animation in her voice. After exchanging a worried glance with Clay, she coaxed, "I put alphabet noodles in the soup."

Abby's interest picked up a bit. "Can I see?"

Clay was sitting on the side of the bed now. After he propped Abby up on pillows, he helped position the tray in front of Abby.

He dipped in the spoon, catching a few of the alphabet noodles. "Open wide."

Abby did, and he spooned the soup into her mouth. She turned her eyes to Celeste. "It's good," she pronounced, and that compliment meant everything to Celeste.

"I can feed myself, Daddy. I'm a big girl." She took the spoon from him and dipped it into the soup. But after a few spoonfuls, she began coughing again.

Clay took the tray and set it on the bedside table.

"We can let this sit for a little while. How about more apple juice?" After a few sips, Abby settled back on the pillows again. Clay plugged in a set of headphones and adjusted them on Abby's ears.

"Maybe she'll fall asleep," he said in a low voice as he and Celeste sat crossed-legged on the floor, their backs against the bed, and picked at their dinners while Abby resumed watching her movie.

"I don't like the sound of that cough," he said.

"Has Abby been sick very much before now?"

"The occasional cold or tummy upset, but nothing serious. This just happened so fast."

Celeste's instincts told her it wouldn't clear just as fast.

"You don't have to stay, you know."

"I know. But I don't want to leave Abby now." She didn't want to leave him, either, to deal with this alone, but she couldn't tell him that.

After a few more bites of dinner, he asked, "Do you want to bunk here tonight?"

"If you don't mind. I can just sleep on the sofa."

His protest came quickly. "Don't be silly. I have a guest room and it's made up." He must have seen the look in her eyes because his brows furrowed, and he asked, "Do you need an explanation?"

"I don't have any right to an explanation."

After one of his leveling looks, he said, "Once in a while I have a client who's come a long way. If I know him or her, and they can't find other accommodations, I let them stay here. If I do that, I take Abby to spend the night with my mother. It's just a precaution. I won't take any chances with her."

"But you said you don't let them stay unless you know them."

"Yes, well...I thought I knew Zoie, didn't I? Appearances can sometimes be deceiving. Anyway, the room's made up, so you can settle yourself in."

"We can take turns with Abby," she suggested, not knowing if he'd go for that or not.

"It probably would be best if we were both able to get a little sleep. So that sounds like a good idea."

"Can I help you change her into pajamas?"

Clay shifted, straightening his legs. "She probably gets tired of me being the only one who takes care of her at night."

"I doubt that."

When he shook his head, a lock of his hair fell over his forehead. "I'm not fooling myself, Celeste. I know a

woman's touch is important. She loves my mom, but…"
He ran his hand through his hair, pushing it back into
place. "I don't know how to explain it. There's a wall
there. Maybe it's my mother's generation. Maybe it's the
fact that I don't think Dad approves of her spending as
much time with Abby as she does. I think that's always
in the back of her mind."

Celeste was distracted by the thick texture of Clay's
hair, his long fingers riffling through it. But this was
important history he was giving her so she forced herself
to focus on his words. "And the reason your dad doesn't
approve?"

His voice low, he answered, "There are quite a few
of them. He never approved of Zoie, so a child of hers
is in the same category. He never approved of the way
Abby came into the world with you as a surrogate. He
believed if Zoie couldn't have children, we should either
go childless or adopt. Like I said, there were so many
reasons. I guess that's his way of looking at things."

"You don't see him mellowing with age?"

Clay almost snorted. "No! He is who he is. He actually
does have a kinder, loving side. I see it with Mom all the
time. But when someone disagrees with him, he's a bear.
She's the only one who has the power to calm him with
a word or a look." He stopped and paused. "I don't know
why I told you any of this."

"Because it could affect Abby."

"Possibly. Or maybe you're just a good listener."

Celeste glanced at Abby and saw her eyes were closed.
She kept her tone soft. "You're Abby's father. I want to
learn everything I can about her. I've missed over three
years of her life. Do you understand how much catching
up I feel I have to do?"

Although they were sitting close together, no part of

their bodies was touching. She realized now that they were both aware of why. One touch could lead to another and then another. The force field that surrounded them, though, seemed to be pulling them toward each other.

Celeste waited for Clay's answer, breathing in the lingering scent of his aftershave, wishing she could push his hair over his brow, to show him she cared. The gray of his eyes seemed to grow more mysterious, the muscle in his neck pulsed. He was so still, she wondered if he was going to respond.

Instead of answering her, though, he asked a probing question. "I understand that you felt like Abby's mother when you were carrying her. When you delivered her. Maybe even when you left here without her. But after the first few months, after a year, did you still feel like her mother?"

"Are you saying I didn't because I stayed out of your life?"

"I'm not doubting, Celeste. I'd just like to know."

Letting her thoughts and feelings spill out to Clay was fairly easy. "The first six months were so hard. I kept telling myself she was your child all along. She was Zoie's little girl. I tried to see myself as a doting aunt, but I knew I couldn't do that then, and I didn't know when I'd be able to. I never stopped feeling like her mother, Clay. Maybe if I'd been a surrogate for a stranger, everything would have been different. But being a surrogate for Zoie, I think I felt even more attached. All the counseling in the world couldn't prepare me for leaving Abby with you, for pretending I wasn't part of who she was."

He leaned closer to her, his voice gentle. "And you never would have told us that."

"No."

They were facing each other, so near their breaths

could mingle…so near a kiss wafted in the air between them. But Celeste wanted more than a kiss—she wanted to be an integral part of her daughter's life.

She took a deep breath, leaned away and rose to her feet. "I'll clean up the kitchen, then we can get Abby ready for bed."

Clay nodded, gathering their dishes onto the tray on the floor. Then he pushed himself to his feet and said, "I'll take this to the kitchen for you."

Celeste watched him leave the room as she sat on the bed beside Abby. She listened to her daughter's breathing, memorizing the sound, exceptionally glad Clay was letting her stay.

Clay knew he wouldn't be able to sleep. However, at two o'clock in the morning he went to his room to try. Allowing Celeste to take a watch with Abby unnerved him. But he was on alert with the baby monitor for every sound, every cough, every sigh his daughter made. Being Abby's father had brought joy and light and love into his life.

But having Abby had clinched the end of his marriage. Except at the beginning, his union with Zoie hadn't brought him joy. It had been difficult living with her discontent, which started when he'd made the decision to launch his guiding service. Zoie had wanted him to work for his father and go on to become a Wall Street wizard. But after working at banking for six months, he'd known he'd get claustrophobia daily if he had to stay cooped up in a building with computers and figures.

Zoie had pretended to be accepting at first. But then she'd tried to convince him to give up guiding in none-too-subtle ways. She'd erase messages from potential clients. She'd give him the silent treatment when he returned from an overnight trip. She'd put MBA information on his nightstand. He hadn't wanted to siphon money from the trust fund his grandfather had left him, so they'd lived on a budget. She'd been especially unhappy about that, too. And when Zoie was unhappy, everyone knew it. After Abby was born, she became even more dissatisfied with her life.

Celeste was *so* different. She seemed to know instinctively how to love Abby unconditionally. Watching Celeste with Abby made his heart ache, and he didn't even know why. She seemed to be everything a mother should be—playful, watchful, attentive, kind. It was kindness that he'd always admired in Celeste.

Always admired. Had he noticed her back in high school? Had he been aware of her as a woman when she visited him and Zoie before Abby was born? If he was honest with himself, he'd started making comparisons between the women after Zoie's affair. Is that why he'd made sure to keep his distance from Celeste?

Although the blinds were closed, the shadows on the walls seemed to shift as a summer wind blew outside, whistling against his log home. He stacked two of his king-size pillows, knowing he wasn't going to get any sleep. The best he could hope for was to still his racing thoughts.

All at once, he went on alert. He heard Celeste murmuring to Abby, "Sit up, honey. Let me rub your back."

Then he heard Abby break into a fit of coughing. He was off his bed and down the hall.

When he reached Abby's bedside, Celeste had her cell phone in her hand. "I think we should call 9-1-1. She's having trouble breathing."

Abby's congested coughing started again.

He took out his own phone and speed-dialed emergency services.

Celeste arrived at the Miners Bluff Urgent Care Medical Center five minutes after the ambulance that had transported Abby with Clay riding along. She was scared, her heart pounding madly. Miners Bluff didn't have a hospital per se, but this twenty-four hour facility was well-staffed. Anyone with an illness that couldn't be handled here was transported to the hospital in Flagstaff.

The double glass doors automatically slid open as Celeste rushed toward them. When the paramedics had arrived, they'd given Abby oxygen and hooked her up to an IV line. Was this just a bad chest cold? Could she brew pneumonia that quickly? What would it take to turn this around?

Spotting Clay, she ran toward him. He looked tortured beyond measure as he retrieved his insurance card from the receptionist. "They took her back. They're doing a breathing treatment, but I had to check her in."

A tall, lean doctor with ocean-blue eyes came from the door behind the desk and stopped when he saw Clay. His name tag read Dr. Adam Cooper.

"Adam. Thank God, you're here. Can I go back there and be with her?"

"Sure you can. She's scared and you can probably calm her down for us." He eyed Celeste for a moment, then asked, "You were her surrogate mother?"

Celeste knew Clay had called Dr. Cooper after his 9-1-1 call. Her own name must be in Abby's history, and her pediatrician knew all about it. That made everything easier.

As if Clay just realized how Celeste must be feeling,

too, he took a deep breath, then held out his hand to her. "Come on, I'm sure she'd like to see both of us."

The warmth of Clay's hand enveloping hers almost brought tears to Celeste's eyes. She fought them and walked side by side with him down the hallway.

As soon as Abby saw Clay, she tried to sit up, but he rushed to her, spoke to her softly and readjusted the oxygen cannula at her nose. "You're going to be okay, ladybug." He lifted his gaze to Dr. Cooper.

"My educated guess is that she has the new strain of flu that's making the rounds. That means it's viral, but I want to make sure she isn't hatching a secondary infection. Her lungs are congested and I ordered a chest X-ray to see just how bad that is. After I have that and results from her blood work, we'll decide where we go from here."

"Is there any reason she should be in Flagstaff instead of here?" Celeste asked.

"I don't believe so, but that's your choice."

Clay stroked Abby's hair. "Let's see what the tests say first."

"That's a good idea," Dr. Cooper agreed.

"C'leste," Abby cried, reaching her hand up.

Experiencing all the feelings of a mom, yet knowing she didn't have those rights yet, Celeste went to Abby and took her hand. "I'm right here. The doctor wants to take some pictures of you. Do you think you can let him do that?"

She bobbed her head. "Come wif me?"

Celeste's gaze went to Clay, and she could see he was struggling with that one. He didn't want to leave his daughter's side.

"This won't take long," the pediatrician assured them. "Fifteen minutes, tops."

Clay finally responded, "Go ahead. I'll make some phone calls. But if she wants me, come get me."

"Of course," Celeste said, trying to assure him this wasn't a competition.

His eyes held hers for a long time, then he leaned down and kissed Abby's forehead.

Celeste spoke to Abby as a technician pushed her gurney down the hall to the X-ray room. She encouraged her to hold her breath as the images were taken. She was by her side again as they returned to the small cubicle, assuring Abby her dad would be waiting for her. As soon as she felt better, they'd all go home.

Well, Clay would be going home with his daughter. She would be going back to Mikala's.

Unless she offered to stay and help...

"How'd it go?" Clay asked anxiously when they returned.

"She did terrific. When they took the pictures, she pretended she was holding her breath in a swimming pool with Nemo floating by."

Clay pulled two vinyl chairs up to the side of the bed. Celeste sank onto one while he lowered himself into the other. They were shoulder to shoulder, arm to arm, leaning forward to Abby. This time neither of them moved away.

As Abby's eyes closed, Clay turned to Celeste. "You've been terrific with her. I suppose we're going to have to look at the situation differently when this is over."

"How so?"

"I guess part of me was hoping you wouldn't be good at mothering, that you'd be just as flighty as Zoie. But you're not. So I have to seriously consider you being a part of her life, not just a visitor who comes and goes."

The lump in her throat seemed to become larger the

longer she looked into Clay's eyes. She was about to tell him that new hopes and dreams were tied up to a life in Miners Bluff, but she didn't get the chance.

Suddenly there was noise in the hall, a man's loud voice, a woman's soothing tones, then Harold Sullivan was standing in the doorway, his piercing gaze targeting his granddaughter. He took in Clay and Celeste sitting by the bed, Abby's IV line and the oxygen.

Without a hello, without asking how his granddaughter was doing, he proclaimed, "We're moving her to Phoenix. I've ordered a helicopter."

Clay rose to his feet. One hand still on his daughter's arm, he stared at his father for a heavy moment before he said firmly, "You and Mom shouldn't be here—you could catch the flu. And you can just cancel the helicopter. Abby's staying right here, Dad, at least for now. I'm her father and I make those decisions."

Clay's father's face drew tight with anger. He took his wife's arm, turned and left the cubicle muttering, "We'll see about that."

Celeste wondered if Clay's adult life had been filled with confrontations like this with his father. She clasped his forearm. "I agree with you. She should stay here."

At that moment, complete understanding vibrated between them, along with something deeper and more elemental. But she knew neither of them would acknowledge that until Abby's crisis was over.

Maybe not even then.

Chapter Seven

"So Clay's with Abby now?" Jenny asked, as Celeste sat in the waiting room of the urgent care center with her cell phone to her ear.

"I felt he wanted time alone with her." Celeste had known Jenny would be up at six caring for the horses. She needed to talk, just as they'd talked back in high school and in the years since.

"Is Clay making you feel as if you don't belong there?"

"I think he was glad I was here. But I know my presence made it harder when his parents arrived." She told Jenny what had happened.

"But Clay didn't back down?"

"No. His dad just always has this need to feel he has the upper hand. It's exhausting for me. I can only imagine what it's been like for Clay dealing with him his whole life."

"So tell me again why you feel Clay needed to be alone with Abby."

"Sometimes I just feel like I'm intruding, like he doesn't trust I'm going to stay and he's afraid Abby will get too attached. *He's* been the one constant in her life."

"You have every right to be there," Jenny assured her.

"Do I? Really?"

"Yes, really. I think you're reacting to something else."

Celeste kept quiet.

"Aren't you?"

"Last night as we sat in her room, watching over her, it felt so...intimate."

"And you don't know if you want that?"

"I don't know if Clay wants it. I don't know if either of us are *ready* for it."

"When you two were dancing at the reunion, something was going on."

"You saw it?"

"Don't sound so horrified. I don't think just anyone could. It was subtle. But I know you and I know Clay. Mikala saw it, too." Jenny hesitated. "This time, you have to follow your heart, Celeste."

"What do you mean?"

"You gave up Abby and you stayed out of her life. You dated that pilot to try to forget about Abby, because you felt time was passing and you wanted more than a career. And I'm sure that wasn't what your heart was telling you to do."

"No, it wasn't," Celeste admitted. "This time I will follow my heart where Abby's concerned."

"But not with Clay?"

"We'll see." After the pause that followed, Celeste asked, "Have you heard from Zack yet?"

"No. He called Silas, though. A lot of good that did. Silas told him he was great, the spring foals were coming along and I was handling a few new clients." She gave a heavy sigh.

"And Zack believed him?"

"Zack wants to believe him so his life in California isn't disturbed. But Silas is participating in fewer activities around here every day and that worries me on lots of levels."

With Jenny's pensive silence, Celeste asked, "Have you heard from *your* father?"

"He called from Wyoming a few weeks ago. I'm really hoping he'll get back here for the holidays this year."

Although Jenny's father had disappointed her over and over again, her friend always hoped things would be different.

"I think I'm going to go back in and sit with Abby, too. I feel now that I'm back into her life, I don't want to waste a minute."

"If I had a child, I know that's the way I'd feel too." Jenny said the words with such heartfelt sincerity that Celeste wondered what was behind that feeling.

"Keep me updated," Jenny told her.

"I will."

Clay's heart rate sped up as Celeste returned to Abby's room. Last night he'd believed the wired feeling was strictly from worry about Abby, but now he knew better.

He'd been awake all night as Celeste had been. They'd talked now and then, sat in the quiet, their thoughts colliding as much as their words when they did speak. It had almost been a relief when she'd left a while ago. He knew she felt his relief and didn't know what to do about it. Too much was happening at once, and he couldn't sort the nuances. He didn't *want* to sort the nuances.

"Has the doctor been in?" Celeste asked as she stood by Abby's bed, looking down at her, stroking her fingers through his daughter's hair.

"No, but she seems to be breathing easier. Maybe that's just wishful thinking on my part."

Celeste watched Abby a few more moments as if counting each breath, as if studying every curve and dimple on his child's face. When she rounded the bed and sat beside him, he noticed she was careful not to let her body lean toward his. They were *both* being so damn careful.

"I could use some coffee," he said gruffly. "I think I'll go find some."

"I could have looked, but—I called Jenny. Talking always helps."

"Sometimes."

"I say the wrong thing too often with you," she murmured.

He leaned forward, set his elbows on his knees and rubbed his eyes. "No, I just pick up the wrong words. I forget you don't use them as weapons."

"Like Zoie? Or your father?" she asked gently.

"Both. Dad's just more blunt about it and I can usually see it coming."

"Why can't he let up with you?"

"I'm not sure. But I think it has to do with his need to control. My mother explained it when he and I butted heads over me not staying in banking. His father had been the great Austin Sullivan. When he'd turned his copper mining shares into real estate holdings, he hopped from one project to the other, making more money with an investment in a mall or a high-rise in Manhattan. My grandmother died when Dad was around twelve, and because his father had so many business interests, he put Dad in a military school. So essentially my father had no control over his life until he was out on his own. Then he made sure he *got* control. Once I was born, he was determined to be around, not to be an on-the-road dad, so he felt he had to manage every aspect of my life. It's an explanation, but it doesn't help when I'm trying to communicate with him, or to remind him his responsibility toward me is over."

"But responsibility as a parent is never really over, is it?"

"You know what I mean."

"Yes, I do. I think you mean he never learned how to let go, and that's a different thing. I mean, for instance, if Abby was thirty and suddenly she lost everything, wouldn't you still feel responsible for her?"

"Of course," he confessed with a sigh. "But that's not the case here. I do have a life. I have money in the bank I've saved, a retirement account, investments, a house and a daughter who makes my life worthwhile. All this in addition to my grandfather's trust fund. So I have trouble understanding why he can't just stand back and enjoy my success."

"Spoken like a son," she said with a soft smile that sent heat through his body.

He pushed himself to his feet. "I'm going to find that coffee."

But before he was halfway across the small room, the door opened and Dr. Cooper stepped inside. "Good morning," he said, crossing to Abby.

Abby's eyes popped open. "Daddy. Thirsty," she mumbled.

Clay looked toward the doctor, and he nodded, as he came over to check the IV.

Clay adjusted the straw in Abby's glass and held it for her so she could drink. She sipped thirstily, then reached up her arms to him for a hug.

"Good morning, baby. I think the doctor would like to look you over and see how you're doing. Okay?"

Instead of agreeing, she reached her arms toward Celeste. Celeste came over and hugged her, too. "Are you feeling better?" she asked softly.

Abby gave her a little smile and a nod, though Clay knew that was more because she wanted to go home than because she might really be feeling better. He could see from Celeste's expression, that not-quite-radiant smile, that she knew it, too.

The doctor took a strip from his pocket and said to Abby, "I'm going to take your temperature again. I'm just going to put this right on your forehead for a little while and then I'll know how you're really doing. Okay?"

She let him place the strip across her forehead. Then he listened to her chest while he waited, checked the glands at her throat, played a game with her with his penlight.

Reading her temperature, he turned to them. "Her fever's down. Low-grade now. I want to keep it that way so I suggest we keep her here until midday. I want to keep her hydrated and give her more IV meds. I'll check her again later. With kids, you never know what's going to happen next. But I think I can predict with some degree of accuracy that she could be going home before evening. Everybody okay with that?"

"Home, Daddy." Those were the words Abby heard.

"Before the moon comes out tonight, you might be going home. Until then, Celeste and I will read to you, or sing to you, or whatever you want to do. Okay?"

"Okay," she agreed. "Can Granny come play?"

"She'll play with you after you feel better."

Adam Cooper headed toward the door.

Clay looked at Celeste, and Celeste looked back, and then they were smiling and hugging with the bonding joy only parents can know when their child is on the mend. The joyful embrace soon became something else. Clay leaned away slightly. Celeste tilted her chin up and met his gaze. He would have kissed her right then and there, but for Abby. And the look in her eyes matched the desire he felt.

As he broke away, Celeste didn't try to hold on. But even as she stepped back, he knew they did indeed have a problem.

They couldn't deny their attraction any longer. So what were they going to do about it?

Clay entered Abby's cubicle to see his daughter sitting on Celeste's lap, ready to go home. He folded her instruction sheet into quarters and tucked it into his jeans pocket. Taking a seat on the bed across from the two of them, he considered how to approach Celeste about a problem he now faced.

Abby coughed a little and laid her head against Celeste's shoulder. If nothing else, her gesture signified that he was doing the right thing.

He said quietly to Celeste, "Are you busy the next few days?"

Her gaze lifted to his. "That depends. What's going on?"

"Adam said it could be a week until Abby's feeling up to par again."

"I suspected that."

"I'm supposed to take a family of three to the Grand Canyon overnight next weekend. Usually when I do that, Mom stays with Abby at the house, but her sister in Tennessee called. Her daughter's planning a wedding and she wants Mom's help. Mom said she wouldn't go but I don't want her to catch the flu and it will be good for her to get away. So how would you like to stay in my guest bedroom for a few days? I thought you could get used to being around Abby more often, and if everything works out, you could take care of her while I go to the Grand Canyon."

Several emotions seemed to pass across Celeste's face. At first, surprise, then delight, then uncertainty. He knew what that uncertainty was about. There was a reason having Celeste in his house for the next week might not be a good idea.

"I'd love to take care of Abby, and I want you to see that you can trust me with her. But I don't want to... complicate our situation, either. Are you sure you want me to stay?"

Oh, he wanted her to stay...on so many levels. But what he wanted and what they were going to do were two different things. "We're adults, Celeste. We can put Abby first. We can get along without doing anything we'll regret. Four days before I leave isn't a long time."

"No, it's not," she agreed brightly, as if he were putting her fears to rest as well as his.

"So you'll come stay with us?" he asked.

"I will," she agreed, her arms hugging Abby just a little tighter.

He knew he wasn't out of the rapids yet. Letting Celeste bond with Abby even more could be a big mistake. But she was obviously committed to forging a relationship with his little girl. How could he get in the way of his daughter's need for a mom?

He asked himself that question again a few hours later after Abby was tucked in for the night and he was showering. It felt odd having Celeste in the house, present at meals, playing with Abby, just being in the next room. She'd set up her computer in the guest bedroom, and he supposed she was working on a project for her business. They didn't seem to know how to act around each other, but she'd decided to take the safest route by disappearing into the guest bedroom for the evening after Abby went to bed.

After his shower, he dressed in shorts and a T-shirt and went into the kitchen for a beer. After he twisted off the cap, he took the longneck bottle out into the sunroom.

He had drawn only a few swigs before he heard Celeste's footsteps in the kitchen. These were the moments he was both anticipating and dreading during the next few days. He was revved up with her staying here, even more revved up when she came within a few feet of him. Now, however, there seemed to be purpose in her step, and she was carrying her laptop.

"Going to work out here?" Two of the windows were open, and a breeze wafted in. She sat beside him on the wicker sofa, and hairs on the back of his neck practically stood on end.

But she kept a few inches between them as she opened her laptop on the glass-top table in front of them. "I'd like to show you something."

"Work you finished for a client?"

"A prospective client," she said with a small, sly smile.

After the laptop booted up, she clicked a few keys.

Suddenly he was looking at a page, a very attractive page with beautiful northern Arizona scenery, along with his logo and photo.

"What's this?"

"If you want an internet presence, I'd like to create a website for you. I was just playing around and this is something I came up with. I used your brochure as a guide."

She clicked one of the dark green buttons along the side of the website. "I've included a page with your bio and qualifications." She reverted back to the front page and clicked another button. "This one lists the available tours you give. Notice that I mentioned you're willing to customize tours to your clients' needs." She clicked on another button. "These are FAQs so it will give clients a basis for information." She pressed another key. "On this one, they can fill in the type of tour they'd like if they want it customized. They can also ask questions and email you the form, or as you've noticed..." She went back to the front page. "They can email you directly from here. I can also set this up if you'd want to do a blog. You know, highlights from the tours you do each week, something like that." She pointed to another icon. "And I can upload info to one of the social networking sites. We can sign you up so clients can follow you if they want."

"I'm amazed. How long did it take you to do all this?"

"A few days. I snatched time here and there. I just finished putting it together tonight. What do you think?"

"I think I've underrated what you do. It's terrific, Celeste!"

"We can also do a couple of well-placed internet ads if you need more business. I'll hook you up to the search engines that matter. It will just make finding you a lot easier for someone who's across the country or in another state. If you have to turn people down for tours, you have to turn them down. That will put your services that much more in demand."

This was another facet of Celeste he'd never seen—a professional, savvy businesswoman.

He sat back on the sofa, staring ahead at the webpage. She relaxed against the cushion, too, and their shoulders touched.

"How much will all this cost me?" he teased.

"I might give you a discount since you're an old friend."

"Old?" he asked, with a raised brow.

She laughed. "Relatively speaking."

They turned toward each other at the same moment. *In* that moment, Clay realized why he'd been hesitant to ask Celeste to stay here. The impact of them sitting alone on the shadowy porch teased his libido, encouraged his hormones to run after one another, tickled restlessness that could make him reckless.

On their way home from the urgent care center, Celeste had stopped at the Purple Pansy to pick up some clothes and necessities. He hadn't thought much of it then, but now he realized these nights were a pajama party of sorts. She was wearing cotton lounging pants, patterned with pink and yellow flowers. Her tank was pink, too, tucked into the drawstring waistband. The outfit was meant to be comfortable, not alluring. Yet to him, it was. *She* was.

Too long without sex, he thought. That's all this attraction was, wasn't it?

Celeste seemed to be as immobilized as he was by the sense of awareness between them, by the palpable rippling of attraction, by the alarm bell reminding them both they had good sense and they'd better not lose it.

"Do you think my staying here is a mistake?" Celeste asked in almost a whisper.

"I think that, at the moment, your being here is a necessity."

"For *Abby*." She obviously wanted to be clear about it.

"And for us. We have to figure out what we're made of, Celeste, if a couple of kisses could throw our lives off track, or if there's something greater that can motivate us to do what we know is right."

"What's right, Clay?"

There seemed to be a hint of challenge in her voice and he wasn't sure where that was coming from. She didn't want to get involved any more than he did, did she?

"Right is being clear about who we are and what we want, and not confusing Abby." He took a sip of beer. "While we were hiking on Moonshadow Mountain, I got the feeling you didn't want to talk about your relationships with men. A woman as attractive as you has had to have had some romantic liaisons."

She was silent, and he didn't understand why until she answered, "Not many. I never felt I needed someone else to give my life meaning. I mean, yes, I wanted to find love. I wanted a family. But I didn't actively search, if you know what I mean."

He found that hard to believe. After all, when Zoie had had an affair, he'd wondered if she'd been searching all along, if she compared every man to him, or vice versa, if they were both to blame for her wandering eye, or just her.

"You look as if you don't believe me."

"I haven't been on the dating circuit since high school,

so what do I know? I guess I thought all single women were on the hunt."

She was already shaking her head. "When I first moved to Phoenix, I worked nonstop in an art supply store to earn money for classes. Then I worked for an employer who didn't understand forty-hour weeks, which was fine because I liked what I was doing. When I went out on my own, I definitely didn't have time for happy hour."

"So you're telling me you didn't date?"

"I'm telling you that I found someone when I least expected to, but it didn't work out."

"You're leaving a lot out."

"I'm not trying to be coy, Clay, but does it really matter?"

She had a point. Did it matter? Yes, for some reason, it did. He wanted to know who she'd been involved with and for how long. "Tell me about it," he requested gently, not wanting to drag it out of her. He wanted her to willingly confide in him and didn't analyze that fact too much.

The lamplight from the side table gleamed in the golden strands of her hair as she revealed, "I met him at a rock-climbing workshop. It was just a one-day class at a gym. Peter was taking it, too."

"Peter." Clay tried out the name, then he decided he didn't like the guy no matter what he did or looked like. "Was he trolling for women?"

"That's why *you'd* take a rock climbing workshop?"

He shot her a quick smile, trying to make the conversation nonthreatening. "I already know how to climb. I wouldn't take a workshop."

She scrunched up her nose at him. "You know what I mean."

Not understanding why Celeste's quiet prettiness hadn't affected him in years past as it did now, he answered truthfully. "I don't know. I never thought about it. What did he do for a living?"

"He's a commercial pilot. He was great on those rocks...helpful...caring. It wasn't his first workshop."

"He was from Phoenix?"

"Originally from Florida. That's where his family lived. He'd been based in Phoenix about five years."

"So what happened? Why didn't it work out?"

"We dated for over a year. I thought everything was great between us. We weren't engaged yet, but we were talking about moving in together and I thought we would be soon."

Once she stopped and didn't go on, Clay prompted, "But?"

"He had an affair." As soon as the words came out of her mouth, he was sorry he'd pushed her—the pain was visible in her expression. Still, she went on without his prodding. "He met Marie in Italy. I don't know how many times they were together. I didn't want the details. But she became pregnant and he moved to Naples to be with her."

"Whoa."

"That tells you something about what he thought of me, doesn't it?"

Clay couldn't help but move closer to her until their bodies were a whisper apart. "That's *not* true and you have to know it."

Looking away, she bit her lower lip. "No, I don't know it." Her gaze swung back to his. "How gullible was I? How naive? All this happened about the same time Zoie asked you for a divorce and for the next year all I could do was think about the family that I wanted—the fact that I *did* have a daughter and she could be my family if you'd let her."

Ignoring that for the moment, he said, "I guess we both know how to pick 'em."

Celeste's hair rippled over her shoulder as she shook her head and protested, "Zoie loved you, Clay. I know she did. But the two of you were young when you married. And Zoie, she had expectations. You were a Sullivan with a trust fund and a potential career in banking like your father. Along with that, she was headstrong and when she made up her mind, nothing could change it."

"You mean the way I couldn't change her mind about leaving."

"Yes." Celeste hesitated. "Did she ever really bond with Abby?"

More times than he could count, Clay had asked himself the same question. "I don't think so. She hired babysitters. She didn't get along with my mother, but Mom kind of watched over Abby anyway. She'd show up whether a sitter was here or Zoie was here. Zoie didn't like it, but in a way, I felt as if Abby had a guardian angel watching over her."

"Why didn't you let me know?"

Delaying the truth and an admission he didn't want to make, he pushed his fingers through his hair. Finally he confessed, "Because I didn't want to see. What man wants to think his wife can't bond with their child? What man wants to think his wife's unhappy, or that he's not enough?"

Celeste didn't say anything. That was probably better because she couldn't really change the way he felt about his guilt and his regrets.

"Zoie did *try* to be a mother," Clay said, remembering. "She'd carry Abby around in one of those slings. She cared for her—her physical comfort, I mean. At first I thought she had some kind of depression, and I urged her to talk to her doctor. I don't know if she did or if the cloud passed on its own. After about six months, she perked up, bought new clothes, used makeup again, started having lunch with friends. But I know now she wanted to see the world and she was stuck in Miners Bluff. She was stuck with a child who wasn't the center of her universe."

"But Abby's the center of *your* universe," Celeste reminded him.

"Since the day she was born."

"Do you think Zoie could have been jealous of Abby?"

"I don't know what Zoie was and I'm tired of thinking about it. She's moved on to the life she wants and I have a life I'm satisfied with."

"But is it enough?" Celeste asked, and he didn't quite understand the questioning look in her beautiful green eyes.

"It's enough. Why would I ever want to put myself or Abby through that kind of wringer again?"

After a long silence, Celeste quietly asked, "Do you still think she's bonding with me because I look like Zoie?"

He didn't want to hurt Celeste, but he had to be honest with her. "Your looking like Zoie might have triggered familiar memories, so you weren't a stranger. But I also think she senses something about you, a type of caring she hasn't exactly received from a woman before, not even from Mom. So she's very comfortable with you."

"Has she had any more bad dreams?"

"Not since you arrived. But I don't think we can read

anything into that. They've been sporadic." He didn't want to read anything into that because of what it would mean.

"I'm glad I'm here, Clay. I'm glad you invited me to stay."

"Anything for Abby."

Celeste sat forward and he did, too. He nodded toward the website. "If you do this for me, we need a formal contract. I'll pay you."

"Clay, no."

"That's the only way I'll let you set it up."

She thought about it. "If you pay me, I'll just put the money aside for something for Abby."

"That's your prerogative."

"Do you need the website?" she asked.

He shrugged. "I can always use more business. I thought about taking on a partner. That could give me more time at home. The website and the added exposure would be a jump start toward that end."

Celeste didn't say what they were both probably thinking—that a partner in *life* as well as business could make things easier, too. But he wouldn't even consider that right now. One failed marriage on his ledger was quite enough.

Celeste looked out the window at the sliver of a moon, glowing with silvery light. "I'd forgotten about late summer nights like this in Miners Bluff. We have them, but it's so hot there. I love the changing seasons here. In Phoenix, it's like one big season."

They were both gazing at the moon now, shoulder to shoulder, thigh to thigh, heat to heat. If he put his arm around her, he didn't think she'd move away. But putting his arm around her, kissing her again, was *not* a good idea. He needed to keep the atmosphere light, needed to distract himself from her sweet scent, her peachy skin, the heat of her body beside his.

Reluctantly, he took his gaze from the moon and set it on the laptop screen. "I really do like this, Celeste."

"Good." That one word seemed a little wobbly to him, but he couldn't be sure.

She tapped a few keys and closed down her computer, then she shut the lid. "I'd better turn in. I'm sure Abby will be up early."

He stood and so did she. They walked into the kitchen together. He glanced around again to look anywhere but at her and saw the message light blinking on his phone.

He gestured to it. "I'd better check my messages. Clients could be calling to change plans."

Celeste didn't move away, he realized, because this could affect *her,* too. He didn't mind if she listened. It wasn't as if there'd be anything personal. However, the first one was from his father. "Clay, give me a call when you get a chance. I need to discuss something with you."

Clay didn't comment, and he knew he didn't have to. He and Celeste exchanged a glance, and she gave him an understanding smile.

The second message was from a client who wanted to discuss the itinerary on his tour the following week. Clay took a pen and pad out of the drawer and made a note. The next message was from a potential new client, and Clay jotted down the numbers.

Celeste began to head down the hallway when the final message played. The voice was familiar, one neither of them would soon forget.

"Clay, it's Zoie. I'm traveling but I need to talk to you.

I lost your cell phone number. I'll try to call you when I get to Cannes. I hope you and Abby are well."

The click after Zoie's call was a resounding noise in the room. Before Clay could even consider what it meant, Celeste had walked away. He heard her door close and wondered what in the hell she was thinking.

Chapter Eight

On Friday Celeste answered the ring of Clay's doorbell and said to Violet Sullivan, "Come on in. Clay went into town to buy supplies before he leaves this afternoon."

Clay's mother was dressed in a pale lilac linen suit and a matching handbag. A driver waited in a luxury sedan outside to take her to the airport in Flagstaff. "I just wanted to stop in and say goodbye and make sure everything was all right here. Is Abby resting? I've really missed her."

"She has more energy every day. She's playing with her dollhouse in the sunroom. I'm sure she'll be glad to see you, too."

For a moment, Violet looked as if she wanted to say something. Instead, she headed through the great room and kitchen's dining area. Celeste followed, wondering what Violet thought about this whole arrangement. Could Clay's mother possibly approve?

When Abby saw her grandmother, she ran to her with open arms and hugged her around the knees. "Granny! Granny! C'leste is here."

In spite of her impeccable outfit, Violet crouched to her granddaughter and gave her a hug. Then she looked toward Celeste. "I know she is. Are you happy about that?"

"Happy, happy. She's gonna stay wif me. Daddy's showing people the big hole."

Violet laughed. "I see."

"Two moons," Abby said, holding up two fingers.

"Two moons?" Violet asked, needing clarification.

Celeste explained, "I told Abby that her dad would be gone for two moons and we'll cross the days off on the calendar."

"That's a good idea. I wish I had thought of it. I'll remember that the next time Clay goes away and I'm taking care of her."

"Play wif me?" Abby asked Violet.

"I don't have much time, honey, but next time I come I'll play. I promise. Can you play with your dollhouse a little bit while I talk to Celeste?"

"Okay," Abby said with a bit of disappointment. "C'leste will play wif me after you go."

Violet's smile was filled with a grandmother's love. "I'm sure she will."

Her attention now focused on her dollhouse, Abby dropped down on her knees in front of it and began taking everything out.

The two women went to the corner of the room. With a studied glance, Violet asked, "How do you feel about staying with Abby?"

"I feel good about it. I love being with her, taking care of her."

"Clay told me how you've helped nurse Abby. Zoie wasn't very good at that kind of thing, at...nurturing. I think Clay is surprised that you are." After some hesitation, Violet asked, "Are you here for a reason other than Abby?"

There was something about Clay's mother that Celeste had come to trust. She hoped she wasn't being naive or gullible. "I was worried about Clay, too. The divorce had to be excruciatingly hard. Being a single dad with a daughter isn't easy, either."

"Zoie hurt him badly," Violet admitted.

"I know."

Violet scrutinized Celeste. "I hope you're the type who sticks around."

Celeste didn't know if Clay's mother was talking about sticking around for Abby or for him. So she merely said, "I know I've only been here less than two months, but I'm beginning to feel like Abby's mom. I'm learning what being responsible for her means. I have a long way to go. If Clay will let me, I want to be here for her as much as I can."

"And for Clay, too?"

There it was, the direct question. What should she say? "I don't know what's going to happen between us next."

Violet nodded.

Maybe because she wanted Violet's approval, maybe because she wanted to feel connected to Clay's mother in some way, Celeste confided in her. "There was a message on the machine when we returned from the medical center with Abby on Monday. It was Zoie."

"What did she want?" Violet's tone had taken on haughty disapproval.

"She didn't say. She was traveling and said she'd call back again."

"What would you do if she came back here?"

This was something Celeste had thought about—a lot. "I know you believe Clay and Abby are better off without her, but as Abby gets older, we're going to have to explain all of this to her. If Zoie wants to stay in contact with her, I'm not sure that's something we should discourage."

Violet looked troubled. "Oh, Celeste. You can't believe she'd be good for Abby."

Maybe sharing her reasons would help Clay's mother understand. "Zoie and I never knew who our father was. Mom admitted when we were older that some of the rumors about her were deserved. But I always wished I knew. I always wished I could find him." She sighed. "That hole can't ever be filled. With Abby, it can be. She'll have me and I'll be here if she needs me. I believe she'll eventually want to know who Zoie was and who Zoie is. I think cutting her off from Zoie could cause resentment and anger later."

Violet moved her purse handle from her right wrist to her left. "Have you discussed this with Clay?"

"No, but at some point I'm sure it will come up. I'll tell him what I've told you. I'm just tossing it out there as a consideration. There's no road map for this kind of thing. But if we keep Abby's interests front and center, I think we'll all do the right thing."

Clay's mother looked doubtful. "Even Zoie?"

"We'll know if she's not thinking about Abby first."

"So you're aligning yourself with *us?*" Violet seemed surprised at that.

"I guess I'm saying maybe there shouldn't be us and her. What one of us does will affect the whole family, especially Abby."

"And just what if Zoie decides she wants to be Abby's mother again and pushes you out?"

Straightening her shoulders, glancing at the little girl who would forever be close to her heart, Celeste took a deep breath. "She's not going to push me out."

Violet glanced over at her granddaughter, who was absorbed in her play, talking to her dolls, rearranging furniture. "I'm glad I stopped in today."

Celeste didn't know if she was glad or not. Only time would tell.

Violet called to Abby. "I'll see you soon, honey." She blew her a kiss and caught one in return. "I can let myself out. Make the most of your time with her. It's very precious."

After Violet left, Celeste worried that she'd said too much. Yet wasn't honesty always the best course to take?

"Are you nervous?" Clay asked Celeste an hour later as Abby sat on her booster chair finishing her lunch.

"I don't think nervous is the word," she responded. "I can cope with almost any situation. But what if Abby wakes up in the middle of the night missing you? Then I wonder what I'll do."

"What *would* you do?"

Celeste thought about it. "I'd rock her and sing to her and read to her or stand on the top of my head if I had to to convince her everything would be okay until you got home."

Clay had to smile. Celeste seemed to know what to say to ease his anxiety. "As I told you, I'm not going to have cell phone service where I'm going."

"I know, but I have a network, too, Clay. Mikala is a therapist and knows kids. Jenny teaches children how to ride, and she said I could call her day or night, too. On top of that, I have the number of Abby's pediatrician. We'll be fine."

Clay's cell phone buzzed. He took it from his belt and studied the caller ID screen. He frowned, not sure if he wanted to take it or not. "It's Dad," he told Celeste. "I'd better take this since he won't be able to reach me for a couple of days."

She nodded and returned to Abby's side, asking her if she wanted more milk. He heard his daughter say instead, "More juice please," and he smiled, knowing he was going to miss her high voice, her arms around his neck at bedtime.

Stepping out into the sunroom, he answered his phone. "Hi, Dad. What's up? I'm on my way out."

"Yes, I know you are. That's why it was paramount that I reached you before you left. You didn't stop in or call about the meeting I wanted to have with you."

"There just hasn't been time."

"I don't like the fact that you're leaving Abby with Celeste. I definitely don't like the fact that Zoie called."

"Just how did you find *that* out?"

"Apparently Celeste told your mother, and of course she called me on the way to the airport. *She* keeps me informed."

Clay didn't know whether to be put out at Celeste or not. What had she and his mother been discussing?

"Well? Did she call back? Is she trying to get more money out of this?"

"She hasn't called back. I have no idea what she wants, if anything. She could simply be trying to make contact before the second half of her divorce settlement is finalized. This isn't your concern, Dad. It's mine. How many times do I have to tell you that?"

"You made a mess of your life with her."

"I have Abby. She's not a mess. I have to meet my client in fifteen minutes and need to get going."

"Didn't you ever stop to think that Celeste could run away with your daughter?"

That made Clay stop and consider the past few days. "The thought ran through my head, but I don't believe Celeste would do that."

"And what's that belief based on?"

Gut instinct. But he wasn't about to tell his father *that*. Harold Sullivan would scoff at the idea. "She's solid, Dad. She's not like Zoie. She understands Abby and what she needs. She understands that Abby needs *me*. Right now she wants to be involved in Abby's life. She wouldn't want to be chased across the globe or hunted down— because that's what I would do if she took Abby into the next county without my permission, let alone across the state line."

"I think you're foolhardy to trust anything about her."

"Just as I was foolhardy in starting a guiding service and making a success of it?"

Silence met his challenge until his father warned, "You're going to be sorry."

"At some point, you're going to have to stop thinking of me as a teenager you can mold into who you want, and deal with me as an adult. I've got to go now. Abby will be fine. I'll give you a call as soon as I get back. Don't worry."

"Famous last words," his father muttered, then ended the call.

Clay just shook his head and went back to the kitchen, where Abby was dipping tiny pieces of fruit Celeste had cut up into yogurt and popping them into her mouth. He motioned to Celeste to join him in the hall so his daughter couldn't overhear.

Celeste leaned down to her, said, "Finish your fruit and I'll be right back," and came to meet him. "Is anything wrong?"

"Not really. Just Dad's usual machinations. But I do have a question. Why did you tell my mother about Zoie's call?"

Celeste's cheeks turned pink, and she looked like a deer caught in the headlights. "She told your dad already?"

"Apparently."

"I'm sorry. I thought you'd tell her yourself. I did it…" She paused for a moment. "I did it because I want your mother to trust me. It led into a discussion about what would happen if Zoie came back, and I was taking over her place in Abby's life."

"What *would* happen?"

"Your mom thought I'd try to keep Zoie away, but I don't believe that would be best for Abby. Some day Abby will have to know the truth. If we keep Zoie from her, that could cause even more emotional upheaval for all of us."

"I can't believe you and my mother discussed this."

"Why? Because she disapproves of me? Because I'm still not the woman she'd choose for Abby's mother? Maybe not the woman you'd choose to *be* Abby's mother?"

"Celeste…" He didn't think that. In fact, chemistry between them aside, she'd make a terrific mom.

"Look, Clay, I know this isn't easy for anybody. Maybe I shouldn't have told your mom about Zoie's call. I'm sorry if that puts you in an awkward position. But at some point we all have to be honest about what we want and what we intend to do."

Clay's attraction to Celeste was growing by leaps and bounds, hour by hour, minute by minute, and right now, listening to her stand up for what she wanted and what she thought Abby needed, his desire for her became a living, furious thing.

He took her arm and pulled her deeper into the shadows of the hall. "You want me to be honest about what I want? I want *you*. I go to bed at night wanting you, and wake up wanting you, and I'm damn tired of trying to ignore it."

Sliding his arm around her, he nudged her close, close enough that he could look into her eyes and search for deception or manipulation or a plan to carry off his daughter to another part of the world where he couldn't reach her. Yet he couldn't see any of that. All he saw mirrored was his own confusion, his own need, and passion just begging to be tapped.

"Clay?" she asked, assuming *he* had some of the answers.

He only had one. He dipped his lips to hers, pressed her into his body and searched her mouth with his tongue. Tiny explosions seemed to go off all over, and he knew he'd lit desire that couldn't be satisfied here...or now.

Tearing away, he pressed his fingers to her swollen lips. Then he went to the kitchen to say goodbye to his daughter. After hugs and kisses and a promise to bring her a stone from the Grand Canyon, he ruffled her hair, picked up his keys, blew her a last kiss and went to the door.

In the hall, looking recovered now from their kiss, Celeste asked, "If Zoie calls, do you want me to talk to her?"

"She's your sister. That's up to you."

As he strode to his SUV, he knew the future had never been more uncertain. He was suddenly glad he had a couple of days away to put the puzzle pieces together.

Jenny wore a straw hat with a huge yellow ribbon to Abby's Sunday afternoon tea party. Mikala's pink bonnet had a smaller brim and tied under her chin. Celeste had adorned her hair and Abby's with daisies from the garden for the occasion as they all sat in the sunroom, cross-legged on the floor, enjoying the warm September afternoon, laughter and each other's company. Entranced with playing dress up, Abby had donned a tiara along with her flowers.

She hugged Lulu close and looked up at Celeste. "Daddy coming home soon?"

She'd asked the question about ten minutes before, and Celeste knew that was her own fault. Before he left, Clay had told her he expected to be home around three on Sunday, and she had let that slip to Mikala while they talked over fruit and milk. Abby had picked it up right away.

"I'm not exactly sure how soon, but I'm hoping before dark."

Jenny said helpfully, "I saw sewing cards on those shelves over there. Would you like to do that for a while? I love to sew."

Abby nodded, jumped to her feet and in her little silver dress-up Mary Janes, went to the shelves for the sewing cards.

"She misses him," Celeste said.

Mikala empathized. "You know that doesn't have anything to do with whether or not she likes to be with you."

"Oh, I know. We've had a wonderful time. I'm so glad Clay trusted me enough—"

Celeste heard a sound in the kitchen. Clay appeared, dusty from the top of his wide-brimmed hat to his well-worn boots. He didn't look happy.

Yet the frown slipped from his face as he spotted Abby and the three women. After a hi and an acknowledging nod to all of them, he scooped up his daughter and gave her a breath-squeezing hug. "Hi, there, princess! Don't you look gorgeous. I'm home."

"I see you," Abby answered, as if what he'd said was obvious.

He laughed heartily, and Celeste could see the lines drop away from his face. "Do you know how much I missed you?"

Abby held her arms out wide. "This much."

"Ten times more than that much."

After a last loving look at his little girl, Clay lifted his gaze to Celeste. Pulsing vibrations seemed to ripple between the two of them as sudden silence descended.

Jenny cleared her throat, then asked, "How was your tour?"

He broke eye contact with Celeste. "It was fine until we met up with a reporter in the Village."

The intensity and simmering desire in Clay's look unsettled Celeste as she thought about the settlement near the south rim of the Grand Canyon where there were lodges, a general store and viewpoints for one of the most beautiful wonders on earth.

"What happened?" Mikala asked with genuine interest.

"A Phoenix network was taping a segment about the end of the tourist season and ran into us. The group I was with was still on an adrenaline rush from everything they'd seen and done. When the reporter asked them questions, they bubbled over with enthusiasm. So now she wants to do an interview with me and maybe even go on one of my tours. I agreed to meet with her at five o'clock at the Feather Peak Diner. I checked it out with Frank Stone, Noah's dad. He's managing it now for Noah's grandmother. He said when the interview airs it might bring more customers in."

Clay's gaze went to Celeste again. "I thought maybe you and Abby could come along and get something to eat. It shouldn't take more than half an hour. Do you think Abby's ready for a meal out? She looks and sounds as if she's back to normal."

The question for Celeste was—was *she* ready for a meal out with Clay? As long as she focused on Abby, she'd be fine. "Abby seems completely recovered—no coughing, no fever and she's been playing nonstop."

"Just what I wanted to hear," he said, giving Abby another squeeze, tickling her, then setting her down on the rug. He checked his watch. "I'm going to have to get a quick shower and change." Then he asked Celeste, "Could I talk to you in the great room for a minute?"

"Abby was just going to show us her sewing cards," Jenny slid in easily. "Go ahead." She exchanged a look with Mikala, and Celeste knew what all that was about. She was sure they could sense the high-velocity attraction that had zipped back and forth between her and Clay the moment he'd strode into the room.

Once in the great room, Clay got to the point. "I don't want to take advantage of you. I know you're here for Abby, but you still have a life. If you mind going to dinner tonight, I can figure out something else."

Although he was thinking of her—and she appreciated that—she also wondered if he was distancing himself by giving her an excuse not to go. "I don't mind, Clay, really."

"Will you stay again tonight?" he asked.

"I don't have any place more important to be. We have to figure out what comes next."

He seemed to consider that. "Did Zoie call?"

"No."

"That doesn't surprise me," he muttered. Then he took a step closer to her, definitely into her personal space. "Abby seems happy. Thank you for staying with her. Thank you for acting like the mother Zoie never was."

"I'm not acting, Clay."

Reaching out, he ran his thumb over her cheek, so tenderly she wanted to cry. "I'm beginning to realize that," he said in a low voice. Then he cleared his throat. "I've got to shower. I'll help you get Abby ready when I'm finished."

Celeste watched him walk down the hall, thinking about the touch of his finger on her cheek and just what might happen later tonight.

Clay dropped down beside his daughter in her booster seat in a booth at Feather Peak Diner and stole one of her French fries. "I'm glad that's over."

Celeste knew Clay wasn't one for the spotlight. He did everything to the best of his ability and didn't expect an award for it. Celeste had watched the taping of the interview from across the room, and knew every woman in the audience would think Clay was as sexy as she did, and many men would want him to take them into the wild, rafting or fishing. "This interview could be important to you."

"That's why I did it."

Alicia Hancock, the redheaded news reporter who had

interviewed Clay, stopped at their table. "Are you sure you won't let me capture your daughter on tape?"

"Positive."

The reporter looked pointedly at Celeste.

Clay introduced the two women but didn't go any further than that.

"In the interview, you said you were a single dad. Is that going to change anytime soon?" Alicia probed.

"You know I want to keep this about what I do for a living, not my personal life."

"It's a lot more interesting if you give me something juicy to work with."

"No."

The reporter glanced at Celeste again. "I told you I know you're divorced."

Clay held up his hand. "Stop right there. If you want to follow me around on my fishing trip next week, we don't go there."

She gave an exaggerated sigh. "Okay, I understand. But when I do the lead-in, I'm going to mention your great-grandfather and how he founded Miners Bluff."

"I have no problem with that."

"All right then. The crew and I will meet you and your party outside Sedona Thursday morning."

"You've got it."

"You're not going to fight me every step of the way while we try to follow you, are you?"

"That depends. You can't make a lot of noise when I ask for quiet, and you can't ask questions that don't have to do with the trip and the guiding business."

"You are *such* a tough sell."

Clay gave the reporter a take-it-or-leave-it expression.

"I'll see you on Thursday," she said with a shake of

her head and a wry smile. Then she crossed to her crew and exited the diner.

Celeste eyed Clay thoughtfully as Abby dipped another fry in ketchup and offered it to her dad. He took it between his lips, then frowned. "I think I need some hot food. Cold ketchup and fries isn't my idea of dinner." He raised his hand to call the waitress.

"Did she ask you other questions you didn't want to answer?"

When Clay went silent, she knew that had been the case.

Finally he responded, "I had her stop the tape at one point."

"Why?" Celeste wanted to know.

"We were talking about the demands of the guiding business."

"Did that get personal because of Abby?"

"She wanted me to step into that juicy territory of the divorce. She asked if long hours and nights away were hard on a family life...hard on a marriage."

"And you didn't answer?"

"No."

Abby wiggled in her booster seat. "Go?"

Clay dropped his arm around his daughter's shoulders. "If you can color while I eat my dinner, maybe we can stop at the Double Scoop for ice cream afterward."

Not knowing how long the interview would take, Celeste had brought a bag along with a coloring book, crayons and one of Abby's favorite puzzles. Now she took the coloring book and crayons from the bag and set them in front of Abby.

"Can I get choc-o-late ice cweam?" Abby asked with a glint in her eye.

"You can have any kind you want."

The waitress came to the table to take Clay's order as he helped settle his daughter with crayons and a coloring book.

Afterward, Celeste wanted to return to their discussion. Clay needed to understand the breakup of his marriage *wasn't* only Zoie's fault. "Did you know how much Zoie missed you when you were gone?"

He looked surprised. "She had interests of her own. After we married and she stopped working, she met friends for lunch…went shopping with them. In good weather, she played tennis. In the winter she worked out at the gym." He ticked off her activities as if he'd gone over them in his head before.

"After you began your guiding service, she missed you, Clay. She'd expected you to have bankers' hours and a lot more time for her."

With a frown, he looked Celeste directly in the eye. "Zoie wouldn't have been satisfied with me being a banker, either. Not here. Her goal for me was to become a financial guru on Wall Street. She wanted to move to New York City. She wanted me to leave everything I loved behind."

"You both had expectations and dreams," Celeste returned quietly.

"It took us a long time to realize we were very different. Those years before we married were filled with high school passion. But then adult life hit us and we seemed to break apart because we had very different perspectives on what gave life meaning." He glanced at Abby and kept his voice low. "But I wasn't the one who strayed. I wasn't the one who kept silent and stewed and resented."

So true. Yet another facet of their relationship was clear, too. "Tell me something, Clay. Were you away as much as you were for the business you were building or because you were trying to escape something in your marriage?"

As soon as Celeste asked the question, she knew she'd gone too far.

With a steely look, he asked angrily, "You're always going to be on your sister's side, no matter what she does, aren't you?"

"That's not true. I'm just trying to see both points of view."

"If you want both points of view, I'll give them to you. I stayed, she left. I accepted responsibility, she shirked it. I remained faithful, she didn't. Those are the facts no matter whose point of view you're dissecting."

Since Clay had ordered the special of the day, his dinner came quickly. The waitress set the platter on the table, telling him to be careful because the dish was hot.

The dish wasn't all that was hot, Celeste thought, watching Clay attack his meatloaf as if it were the enemy.

His anger told her something important—that the wounds from his marriage weren't healed.

Did the two of them even have a chance?

Chapter Nine

Clay knew he had too much pride. That was why he hadn't been able to let go of a failing marriage. It's why he'd stayed with Zoie after her accident, recovery and confession of her affair, why he'd suffered through sharing details of their marriage in counseling sessions. He'd had to *prove* something and live up to his vows. But pride *had* driven him. Tonight his pride had possibly hurt Celeste, and he regretted that. But he didn't know what to do about it. They'd gone for ice cream and taken a walk in the park. All that time, unresolved feelings had pulled taut between them.

Now Abby was in bed, Lulu and the doll Celeste had given her tucked under her arm, her eyes already closed. Celeste had left the room so he could say a final goodnight.

"Good night, ladybug." He kissed his daughter on the forehead, wishing life was simpler for them all.

When he exited Abby's room, he heard Celeste moving around in the guest bedroom. He headed that way and stopped at the open door.

"What are you doing?" Her overnight bag was on the chair, and she was packing the few things she'd brought along and hung in his closet.

"You're home and I think it's time I go back to Mikala's." She didn't meet his gaze as she answered him.

So *she* had a healthy dose of pride, too. Why not? A man had trampled her self-esteem recently, and she wasn't going to let Clay do it. He applauded that. But damn it, he didn't want her to leave.

After he stepped deeper into the room, he stopped beside the antique rocker. "Abby likes having you here."

"I like to be here with her. But I don't think you really want me here, and I don't want to create conflict for her."

She hadn't stopped packing, and now he took hold of her arm, relishing the silk of her skin against his fingers. "You're wrong."

She faced him, toe-to-toe, defiance in her green eyes. "Why do *you* want me here, Clay? For Abby? To make life easier for you?"

"Easier? You've got to be kidding. Every time I look at you, I get turned inside out. Something sparked between us the night of the reunion and I'm trying not to react to it. But I guess some things we simply have no control over."

"We always have control," she maintained stubbornly, but he could see from her expression that she didn't fully believe that, either.

"Not always. Do you know why I was so sharp with you tonight at the diner?" He released her arm.

"Why?"

He guessed she'd already asked herself that question and come up with several answers. "Because I don't like to think about my marriage and my divorce. I'm tired of rehashing and analyzing it. Do you think I don't know that I'm to blame, too? Do you think I don't know that by trying to prove to both Zoie and my father that I could be successful, I broke us apart? When we went to counseling, she never blamed me but she did say she was lonely. She *did* say our marriage wasn't what she'd expected it to be."

Celeste waited, and he knew what she was waiting for. "I made a mistake asking Zoie to marry me. I was caught up in young male lust and our marriage wasn't what *I* expected it to be, either."

"I'm sorry," Celeste said.

So many emotions rose in him, he didn't think he could name any of them. "I don't want you to be sorry. I want *you* to forget you're Zoie's sister. *I* want to forget that I was in a marriage that felt more like a prison than a partnership. And I want you to forget that pilot and what he did to you and go back to being the trusting girl I once knew."

"I'm not a girl anymore," she said so softly he almost missed it.

"Like I don't know that," he muttered with a humorless laugh as his body reacted to her, to the scent of her, to the desire in her eyes.

Slipping his hand under her hair, he nudged her to his body, lifted her chin with his other hand and settled his lips on hers. He'd missed her while he'd been gone. When he'd returned, seeing her again had been like a kick in the gut. It had been a blow that had startled him. This was Celeste, a woman unique in her own right. While he'd lain in his cabin, he'd dreamt of her, awakened sweating and wanting her. Now he wanted her even more. He forgot about the past and the future, and gave in to the need that had been building since their dance in the high school cafeteria. He needed a woman's touch—Celeste's touch—and he needed to touch her in such an elemental way that a kiss couldn't begin to express it.

He felt the same deep fervor from her as her tongue sought his, as they played back and forth, as their kiss became deeper and longer and wetter. He'd meant to apologize to her, but now instead, he wanted to give her pleasure like she'd never known. He meant to satisfy them both so this desire was slaked, so they wouldn't have to deal with it again, so they'd know what coupling with each other was like and they wouldn't have to think about it. Reaching for her blouse, the silky material slid under his fingertips. He could hardly manage the buttons but finally they were undone, and he was pushing it from her shoulders. Celeste's hand smoothed over his upper arms, then ran down the center of his polo shirt and stopped at his belt.

She hesitated.

Breaking off the kiss, he asked roughly, "Do you want to stop?"

"No. Do you?"

"Hell, no," he said on a breathless sigh that told her how stirred up he was. Then he swore. "I don't have any condoms."

"I have an IUD. I never...I never had it removed."

Had she thought the pilot would come back? Would she have wanted him if he'd abandoned a child? But he didn't want to think about that now. He didn't want to analyze anything. He just wanted to bury himself inside of her and savor the moment. Maybe in that moment, he could shuck responsibility and just enjoy being alive.

"Then let's go at this full tilt, no-holds-barred." Her eyes opened wider, and he saw the acceptance of a fire inside of her that matched the one in him.

Without hesitation now, she pulled his shirt from his cargo pants and reached underneath it. He'd watched her hands before as she'd administered to Abby, as she'd fixed dinner, as she'd pushed her hair away from her brow. Now he felt them on his hair, on his skin. The pads of her fingertips were so soft and light, so erotically teasing as she swirled them around his navel, up the center of his chest, around his nipples. He groaned, feeling as if he was going to explode. How was he going to hold on through this? How was he going to give her the pleasure she deserved?

Focusing on *her,* instead of on what she was doing to him, he convinced her to stop so he could rid her of her blouse. She stood before him as he reached around her and unhooked her bra, letting it drop to the floor. Kissing her again, he palmed her breast until she was rubbing against his hand.

When he bent his head, took her nipple into his mouth, teased and licked, she breathed, "Clay, please."

Lifting his head, he arched his brows. "Please, what?"

She laughed, a free sexy laugh he hadn't heard from her before. "Please let's get naked."

He laughed, too, and set about doing just that. Yet he didn't want to hurry it. He wanted everything to be prolonged and erotic and satisfying.

As his thumb slipped back and forth across her waist, he kissed the hollow at her neck, her shoulder under her hair, took her earlobe into his mouth. Had foreplay ever been this heat-filled, this exciting, ever been this necessary for whatever came next? He was going to follow his instincts with Celeste. What else could he do? He didn't want any of it to be the same as it had been with Zoie.

He could hardly stand the anticipation, yet he didn't want to stop it, either. His self-restraint was taxed to the limit as he let Celeste unbuckle his belt, unsnap his pants and unzip them. She dragged her fingers along his waistband, teasing his navel with her index finger. She slid her hands over his briefs to help his slacks fall to the floor.

"Just you wait," he groaned.

"I'm waiting," she returned with a challenging smile that was so unlike the Celeste he'd known in high school that he had to take a second to really study her. She was beautiful with her face flushed, her hair mussed, her eyes bright and sparkling. How had he missed this kind of beauty that began on the inside and radiated out?

Too involved in desire to answer questions, he pulled her to the bed and tugged her down with him. They fell onto it, laughing. It felt so good to laugh with her, to be so in sync with someone. They reached for each other with exuberance and heat and the desire to please. It only took moments to shed the rest of their clothes. Then they were holding on, kissing, caressing, breathing rapidly and prolonging the inevitable. When Clay tangled his fingers in her hair, she reached for him and stroked him.

"We're going to have a quick ending if you do that for very long," he rasped, right before he kissed her brow and lips once more. He couldn't seem to get enough of her soft skin, her sweet scent, her silky hair. He rolled on top of her and then remembered another woman... another time.

Celeste must have sensed something. "What?" she asked.

"Am I too heavy for you?" Zoie never liked him stretched out full-length on top of her like this.

"Of course not," she answered, looking genuinely surprised. "I love the feel of you all around me."

Arousal took on a whole new meaning as excitement seemed to fire every nerve in his body. "I want to be all around you...inside you...everywhere."

Pulling her hands above her head, he intertwined his fingers with hers. As he kissed her, he rubbed against her and she moved her legs restlessly. He knew what she wanted. He knew what *he* wanted. It was time to satisfy them both.

Suddenly his daughter's voice floated from down the hall. "Dad-dee. Dad-dee! I want a glass of water. Daddee?"

He couldn't believe it. He absolutely couldn't believe it. But he'd forgotten to put a glass of water on her nightstand tonight.

For a moment he rested his head against Celeste's, then he rolled off of her. After a few very deep breaths, he called, "I'm coming, baby. Just a minute." He grabbed his pants. "She probably called more than once and I didn't hear her. The monitor's in my bedroom."

"Do you want me to come, too?"

He glanced at Celeste, saw her lips swollen from his kisses, her cheeks bright from their foreplay. "No, it's okay. I'll take care of her."

Seconds later he was striding down the hall to the bathroom for a glass of water for his daughter...wondering if Celeste would still be naked and waiting for him when he returned.

Celeste could have cried. She'd been on the verge of telling Clay she loved him. How foolish would *that* have been?

Putting her hands to her cheeks, she felt the heat coming off of them and knew her whole body was flushed the same way. She also knew she couldn't wait here for Clay naked, to resume what they had started, what they hadn't finished, because now both of them were probably having second thoughts. That passion-filled storm had erupted so fast neither of them had had time to think. The last thing she wanted was for Clay to come back in here and tell her again what they'd been doing was a mistake.

Going into the bathroom, she splashed cold water on her face, even dribbled some of it over her shoulders. She still felt as if Clay's scent was on her, could feel his kisses on her lips. She shook her head, trying to dispel the illusion, trying to come to terms with the love she was feeling. It wasn't new. It had begun a long time ago. Yes, it had been in infancy then with a high school crush, but it had grown into adulthood now. It only took her a few minutes to dress. She was zippering her overnight case when Clay returned.

He took in Celeste lifting her case to the floor and pulling up the handle.

"Something I said?" he asked with an attempt at humor.

"Is Abby okay?"

"I forgot to put a glass on her bed stand. She's supposed to call me instead of getting out of bed because once she gets out of bed, it will take me an hour to get her back in it. Tonight, she really did just want a drink."

He gestured to the suitcase. "So you're leaving now? You don't want to wait till morning? What about what happened here?" he pointed to the bed, and she felt herself blush.

"If we would have had sex, what would that have meant, Clay?"

He was standing in the doorway shirtless and shoeless, his eyes dark, hot and unsatisfied. He'd never looked sexier. She wanted to run into his arms and stay there forever. But she knew as well as she knew her own name that tonight had been about sex for him. A lack of an immediate reply told her that.

Finally he said, "We would have had a hell of a good time."

"And how would we have looked at each other in the morning?"

"I don't understand, Celeste. We would have been two adults, sharing a night of pleasure."

"I don't do that on a whim, and neither do you. We still haven't figured out visitation, when you're going to let me be with Abby, when you're going to let Abby stay with me. If we had gone through with it, everything would have changed between us. We have to keep some objectivity—"

"Don't you think everything has changed anyway?"

His gray eyes were simmering with what they'd shared and she knew what he meant. But their confusion would have been so much worse if their bodies had actually joined. She just knew it.

He wasn't approaching her. He wasn't trying to win her over with a sensual touch. It was as if he had put an imaginary boundary between them now, too.

She wheeled her overnight case to the doorway. "I'd better go."

He studied her carefully and then moved aside. "What should I tell Abby?"

"That I'll see her in a few days. You can let me know whatever's convenient for you."

"Right now, nothing feels convenient," he muttered.

She continued to the front door, knowing exactly what he meant.

On Wednesday, Clay's mother returned to Miners Bluff. That evening she sat with Clay on his patio, watching the sun drop behind Moonshadow Mountain as Abby played on her swing set. She'd stopped in with a lemon meringue pie her housekeeper had made.

"Dad doesn't like lemon meringue anymore?" Clay asked facetiously.

"Your father's trying to lose a few pounds and I'm trying not to eat sweets. I ate too many while I was away. I had to taste too many suggestions for wedding cakes."

Clay laughed. "Then why did Lila bake the pie?"

"Because she thinks it's part of her job. She likes to bake so I let her."

Clay chuckled. "As good a reason as any. What's Dad doing this evening?"

"Playing golf. I just can't see the point of it. I mean, if he actually walked the greens, he'd be getting exercise. But he rides in that golf cart!"

Again Clay had to smile. "So were you lonely this evening or did you have something specific on your mind?"

"I missed you and Abby. I wondered how her first day at preschool went. Can't I visit my son and my granddaughter without an ulterior motive?"

"Yes, you can. But did you?"

Now it was her turn to smile. "I thought Celeste might still be here," she commented innocently.

"No, she left late Sunday. Abby was unhappy about that."

"What did you tell her?"

"I just told her that Celeste had to go back to where she lives."

"Do you wish she was living here with you?"

"Mom..." he said with a cautionary note.

"All right." She held up her hands. "Off-limits. I understand. Actually I wanted to run something by you."

"Concerning Celeste?"

"Yes. I assume she knows her way around the internet."

"Probably better than I do."

"That's what I thought. Do you think she'd be interested in working with me on a family history project?"

"I don't know. You'll have to ask her."

"I understand that. I just wanted to feel you out first. See how you felt about it. It's Abby's history, too. I think it's time I write it all down—what the families have passed down to each other over the years, stories, history, personal relationships. But I need someone to help with the research. I'm not very computer savvy and I know you certainly don't have time to do it."

"Did you get this idea from the Preservation Society?"

"Yes, I did. And that's another thing. You know I came back for the fundraiser Friday night. Will you be there?"

"To eat overbaked chicken, soggy vegetables and ice cream parfait for dessert?"

She swatted his arm. "Sometimes you sound more like your father than you think."

He scowled at that comparison. He didn't like to think he was anything like his father.

"You have his genes, Clay, there's no denying that. Be proud of your heritage."

He *was* proud of his heritage. He just didn't want

to think he shared some of his father's less admirable traits.

"So you want me at the fundraiser as a show of family solidarity?"

"Something like that. Besides, we haven't done anything as a family in a long time."

He sighed. "I guess I could ask Celeste to look after Abby."

"Maybe you could ask someone else to sit with Abby. She likes Celeste's friends, Mikala or Jenny."

"And why not Celeste?"

"I spoke with Anna and she mentioned Celeste would be coming to the fundraiser."

Clay kept silent. Why was his mother trying to draw Celeste into her project? Was she going to see if Celeste was really going to stick around and become involved in town affairs? Was she suggesting he attend a fundraiser because Celeste would be there?

He had to admit he wanted to see her again. He wanted to be around her.

Should he attend the dinner and fuel the desire that still surged at the sound of her name? Or should he just stay home and take a cold shower?

Late Wednesday night, Celeste had given up trying to sleep and was working on her laptop when her cell phone played a popular song. As she took it from her nightstand and saw Clay's number, she didn't know what to think.

"Hi," she said, modulating her voice so it was calm and even, although she didn't feel that way.

"Did I wake you?"

"No. I couldn't sleep so I'm working."

After a few beats of silence, he admitted, "There's a lot of that going around. I would have waited until tomorrow to call you, but I have to be in Sedona by seven. I wanted you to know Abby has been asking for you."

Guilt washed over Celeste. She'd left so abruptly the other night and for the past few days she hadn't tried to see her. "I should have come over."

"You were waiting to hear from me, and I thought we both needed a little time to cool down."

Cool down. She wasn't sure that was going to happen between them, but maybe Clay could turn his desire on and off.

"Celeste?"

"Yes, I'm here."

"Could you come over tomorrow and spend some time with her?"

"Of course, I can. I told Anna I'd help her prepare for new guests in the afternoon. But I'm free all morning."

"Mom will be here. I have that fishing trip. There's a project she wants to involve you in."

"What type of project?"

Clay explained about research for their family history.

"I'd be glad to help her."

"She heard from Anna you'll be attending the fundraiser Friday evening."

"Yes, I will. Anna's great at subtle arm-twisting. Are you going?" she asked, not knowing if she should.

"Yes. In fact, I called Jenny to see if she'd look after Abby. She said she would."

"I could just stay with Abby and forget about the dinner."

"That's up to you. But Abby is going to have to learn you're a steady presence in her life, even if you aren't there twenty-four hours a day."

"Maybe she needs someone to be with her twenty-four hours a day."

"What are you suggesting, Celeste?"

"I'm not suggesting anything. I'm just saying a sense of security doesn't have anything to do with reason or logic."

He was quiet for a few moments. "We'll have to talk about this, among other things. I can't stop thinking about Sunday night...and you. And maybe the interruption was useful, even though it was damn frustrating at the time."

"Useful because we were making a mistake?" She hoped that wasn't what he was thinking, but she knew it could be.

"Useful so we can both figure out what we want."

She didn't have a whole lot of figuring out to do. She knew now exactly what she wanted. She wanted to explore her feelings for Clay and become a full-time mother to their child. But the road she wanted to take might be very different from the one Clay intended to forge ahead on.

"Are you naked now?" he asked.

"Clay—"

"Humor me. Are you?"

If he wanted to indulge in this game, she had to admit she was willing. "No. I'm wearing a silky nightgown, very much like a slip. It's midnight-blue with lace just covering my breasts."

His silence made her wonder if she'd gone too far... or not far enough.

"Well, I asked. It will be my own fault if I still can't fall asleep."

She smiled. She'd never been a risk taker, but she

realized now she had to take some risks with Clay. "And *you're* wearing..." she joked.

"Briefs. I'm ready to shuck them and jump into the shower. A cold shower."

An excited tremor jumped up her spine—she was able to incite his arousal. She felt desired and wanted and scared.

"I won't get back until late tomorrow night," Clay said after a pause. "The Phoenix news crew will be following me around on the fishing trip."

"Alicia will be lively company."

"Alicia will be a pest. She'd better be quiet when the fish are biting or my clients won't be happy."

"She likes you."

"She's doing her job. She thinks a little chemistry will make the interview better. There *is* no chemistry. So we'll see what happens."

She so wanted to say, *I think I love you, Clay*. Yet she knew, as with having sex, once those words were out or the act completed, neither could be put back into the bottle.

Chapter Ten

As Celeste helped Anna slip loaves of banana bread into her oven on Thursday afternoon, she thought about playing with Abby that morning. Anna was expecting guests around five, and she wanted to be ready for them. Mikala was tied up with students in her studio, so Celeste had offered to help her prepare the third floor guest suite and bake.

Anna Conti had been beautiful in her youth. Her black hair was now steel-gray with some black strands throughout. Her hair was wavier than Mikala's and framed her oval face. She was pleasantly rounded in a way that made hugs comforting.

As Anna measured loose tea into a ball for the kettle to make iced tea, she cast Celeste a sideways glance. "You're awful quiet this afternoon, dear. Is something on your mind?"

After Celeste had lost her mother in her twenties, she

hadn't looked for an older woman to confide in. But Anna was easy to talk to and wise in her advice. "I have so many things on my mind, it's hard to pick just one," she joked.

"But I think one is pressing more than the others, right?"

"Mikala told me you're a mind reader."

Anna laughed. "No, maybe just a *heart* reader. What's troubling you?"

"I saw Abby this morning. I could tell she missed me the past few days. I'm not sure how much time I *should* spend with her."

"You want to be with her all the time, don't you?"

"Yes, I do."

"What would be the perfect solution for you?"

Celeste knew what she wanted the perfect solution to be, but happily-ever-after was a pipe dream, she supposed. Clay's heart was still too wrapped up in the past to give it to her. Yet after the conversation last night, wasn't there room to hope?

When she didn't answer Anna immediately, Mikala's aunt put the lid on the tea kettle and looked at her directly. "You've always had feelings for Clay. I know that."

Surprised, Celeste blurted out, "How do you know that?"

"Oh, Celeste. How well do you think a seventeen-year-old hides her emotions? I saw you look at Clay whenever he and Zoie were around. I heard you talk about him with Mikala. There was always something in your voice. Granted, that might have been a high school crush. But all these years later, with you and Clay both free, I can't help but think those feelings have been resurrected. Am I right?"

"You're too right," she confessed. "The thing is, I don't

know if Clay is free. I think he's bitter and resentful of what happened with Zoie. Besides, I'm her sister."

"That shouldn't matter if he cares for you."

Celeste laid the pot holders on the counter. "Do you really believe that? Even if the gossips talk about us from here to next year?"

"I don't put much store in gossip. Sure, some people in town do. But what matters is whether two people are kind to each other, care about each other and are committed to each other. Don't you think?"

"But we have Abby to think about. This could be so confusing for her."

"I suppose, you being her surrogate mother and all. But do you think it would be any different if a stranger had been her surrogate mother, and Clay had feelings for *her?* Or even if he brought a woman into her life who wanted to *be* her mother? Would it be any less confusing then?"

"Any of it would be confusing for a child. I don't know how we'll ever explain it to her."

"Maybe if you love her enough, the explanations will come later, when she's old enough to accept them."

Wasn't that what Celeste herself had told Violet? It had seemed much simpler when she was standing outside the circle looking in, when she wasn't so personally involved with Clay.

Celeste's cell phone, deep in her jeans pocket, started to play. She'd been carrying it with her in case Clay called. To say he wanted her to sit with him and his family at the dinner? Maybe Violet had already arranged that. Her screen read "Private Caller," and she didn't recognize the number.

Anna said, "Go ahead and take it. I'm fine here."

"I won't be long," Celeste said as she opened the phone. "Hello?"

"Celeste, is that you?"

Startled when she recognized the voice, she answered, "Yes, it is, Mr. Sullivan." She waited. After all, *he* was calling *her*. She had no idea what he wanted.

As if he was uncomfortable with the silence, too, he cleared his throat. "I wondered if you could stop by my office at the bank tomorrow morning."

"Can I ask what this is about?"

"It's about your future and Abby's."

"I see." She didn't want to be rude to Clay's dad. She didn't want to brush him off or give him another reason not to approve of her.

"This isn't something we can discuss on the phone?"

"No, I think it's better if we talk in person."

"Did you have a particular time in mind?"

"Around ten would be good for me. I have meetings in the early morning and lunch with a colleague."

"Ten o'clock will be fine."

Her voice still must have held a bit of uncertainty because he reassured her, "This won't take long, Celeste. I promise."

But as she closed her phone, she had to wonder what Harold Sullivan's promises were worth.

Miners Bluff's town hall was situated across the street from the park and next to the courthouse. The town hall, however, was the older of the two buildings and even had its own small bell tower. Celeste and Zoie had once sneaked up there when they were little to find the big bell that rang at noon every Saturday and at midnight on every holiday. The echo of that bell rolled around the whole town, seemingly going up into the mountains and down into the valley. On that same day, Celeste had glimpsed large rooms used for meetings, mahogany conference tables, the grand stateroom on the first floor big enough to hold election rallies and any town function large enough to need a spacious room. Tonight's dinner was being served there.

But dinner and architectural drawings of the new museum were the last thing on her mind. Unfortunately, Clay's father was front and center, stirring up her thoughts, infuriating her all over again. If she saw him tonight, she was afraid she'd be absolutely rude, turn around and walk in the other direction. She couldn't forget his words once she'd settled in a chair in front of his desk this morning.

"I'll keep this short, Celeste," he'd said. "I know you have things to do, and this might make those things even easier. In fact, you might want to go back to Phoenix to do them."

"Mr. Sullivan—"

"Hear me out."

His tone had given her no choice. But instead of discussing family history, instead of discussing anything, he'd held out a check to her. "What do you think about this, Celeste? Five-hundred-thousand dollars, just for you, to use however you want. Half a million dollars to give your life a boost anyplace you want—as long as it isn't here."

She'd been absolutely flabbergasted. The silence in the room had hung between them as she gathered her thoughts. Then she'd stood, taken the check from him, watched the smile spread across his face as she did, watched it change to a look of dismay and disbelief as she'd torn the check up into tiny pieces and dropped it onto the leather blotter on his desk.

"No amount of money will make me leave Abby."

"If you think you're going to get a settlement in the future like Zoie got, you're distinctly mistaken. If Clay is foolish enough to ask you to marry him, I'll make sure the best lawyer in Miners Bluff draws up a prenuptial agreement that can't be broken. You will not ruin my son's life like your sister did."

"I feel sorry for you, Mr. Sullivan. Because you don't believe in Clay, and because you're so jaded you don't realize I just want to be a mother to Abby. That's all."

He hadn't believed her. She had seen it in his eyes. She had seen it in his anger. He hadn't gotten his own way, and that didn't suit him.

"I know you've refused my offer on an impulse. Think about it. I can write another check. And I wouldn't tell Clay about this if I were you. It would be my word against yours. Who do you think he'd believe?"

Celeste had turned her back on him, frustrated and furious. Five-hundred-thousand dollars to make her forget she'd ever had a daughter. How could he think that was even possible? The problem was she really wasn't sure who Clay would believe. Until she was sure Clay really trusted her, it was best if she remained silent.

Taking a calming breath to regain her composure, Celeste found her way to the name-card table. She'd worn her favorite red dress. Its one-shoulder, full-skirted design was a little shorter than she preferred tonight, but she knew that was the fashion. Her gold high-heeled sandals and matching purse added glamour.

A hostess handed Celeste her name card with her table assignment. She found the table easily, and when she spotted the man already seated there, along with a few other fundraiser guests, she felt disappointed that she wasn't with Clay.

Jesse Vargas rose when she approached the table.

"Is this a coincidence?" she asked, really wanting to know.

He grinned. "You can think of it that way. But since my mother is handling the seating arrangements, you could say I know one of the powers-that-be. She made a little switch for me."

Celeste hadn't seen Clay or his family when she walked in, and it was hard to spot anyone in the sea of faces in the large room. As Jesse held her chair for her, she sat and let him push her in.

"I *am* sorry we didn't get much chance to talk at the Rocky D," she apologized. After her discussion with Clay and watching the movie that night, she'd left.

"So you didn't skip out at Silas's to avoid me?" His dark brown eyes wanted to know the truth.

"Jesse, I—"

"Since I saw you that night, I learned you were a surrogate for Clay Sullivan and his ex-wife."

"She and I are twins."

"I see," he said. "But those vibrations I felt rolling off of you and Clay had nothing to do with the surrogacy, did they?"

When she remained silent, he stopped poking. "All right. You don't spread your business around. I get that. Just answer me one question. If I asked you out, would you accept?"

Jesse was a charming, handsome man who seemed like a nice guy, and she didn't want to be unkind. "It has nothing to do with you, Jesse, but I—"

"Say no more. I understand. We're going to be great friends."

At that she had to laugh. "We might be until we finish dinner."

He chuckled as a few other museum benefactors came to the table and took their seats.

Celeste was halfway through her salad and a conversation with Jesse about how he'd moved back to Miners Bluff not so long ago and how it was changing and growing, when she spotted Clay striding across the room, heading to a table in the far corner. Craning her neck, she could see his parents were seated there. Feedback from the microphone on the stage squealed, and he turned in that direction. When he did, his gaze fell on Celeste... and Jesse.

The lines of his mouth tightened. His jaw became set. He looked at her as if...as if he wanted to kiss her, or at least pull her away from her table toward his.

Suddenly there was a hand on her shoulder. Celeste reluctantly turned and found Anna. "Hi, dear. I'm glad to see you made it. I also see you found a friend."

"That's what I am, everybody's friend," Jesse said with mock disappointment.

Anna laughed. "I'm just glad we have a full house and we sold all our tickets." She patted both Celeste and Jesse's shoulders. "You two kids have a good time."

When Celeste looked up, Clay was no longer standing there. He wasn't seated at the table with his parents, either.

Jesse leaned a little closer to her. "Clay stepped outside. I think he needed some fresh air."

"You're not sorry if he got the wrong impression, are you?"

"I'm sure you'll set him right if he did. In the meantime, tell me about Phoenix."

With a wry smile, Celeste did as dinner was served, although she anxiously felt herself looking for Clay again. She really did have to explain she didn't have a date for this fundraiser. And if he didn't feel the same way she did, she'd have to figure out a way to shut down her feelings for him...again. That might not be so easy this time.

Just as the head of the Preservation Committee approached the microphone after dinner, Jesse covered her hand with his. "I wish I could make you smile more tonight."

He really could be a friend if she wanted that. "You're sweet. I just have a lot on my mind. If you'll excuse me, I think I'll freshen up."

As Celeste left the Great Hall, she nodded to a couple of her classmates. Katie Paladin stopped her, saying they should have lunch together sometime. Noah Stone, looking very *GQ* instead of authoritative in his uniform, said, "I hear you might be looking for an apartment so you can become a permanent resident of Miners Bluff."

At her surprised look, he reassured her, "I haven't been gossiping. My grandmother lost her tenant. Clay mentioned you might be interested."

"Thanks for letting me know, Noah. I might be."

"You know where to find me."

"Yes, I do." She'd heard he worked long hours, spending much more time in his office than his predecessor had. After a few more minutes of polite conversation, she veered down a side hall where the restrooms were located.

She was so intent on her thoughts about Abby, Clay's dad and Jesse's offer of friendship that she didn't hear anyone walking up behind her.

Suddenly Clay was beside her, his hand cupping her elbow. He'd left his suit jacket somewhere and pulled down his bolo tie. His shirtsleeves were rolled up, and his eyes were as cold as gray ice. There was a partly ajar door in the hall, and he pulled her toward it. "Let's go in here. You and I have to talk."

"Clay! It's a supply closet..."

He hit the light switch and shut the door. "Yeah, a perfectly private place. This is about the best I can do right now. You're supposed to be sitting with me and my family."

His tone lit a fuse in her own temper. "And how was I supposed to know that? When I picked up my card, it had Table Four stamped on it. I didn't know until I was seated that—"

"What?"

"That Jesse had his mother switch them."

The ice in Clay's eyes held a glimmer of something else now as he clasped her shoulders and concentrated on her so intently she felt herself flush. "The two of you looked cozy," he noted nonchalantly.

She attempted to explain. "I told Jesse that you and I—" She was having trouble finishing her sentences because Clay was close. She could sense the turmoil in him along with the desire. In this small cubicle, Sunday night came back in vivid detail.

Somehow she found her voice. "Jesse could sense something going on between the two of us. He wanted to find out for sure."

Clay's gaze was searching hers, searching her expression, trying to see right through her skin.

"I don't want to be involved with anyone else," she confessed honestly. She knew Clay had his reasons to distrust women. Would he believe her? If he didn't, how could they ever become involved?

All at once, his expression eased. "All right. I believe you." He took her into his arms and captured her mouth with his.

The kiss was ravishing and left no room for doubt about what Clay wanted. As her breasts pressed against his chest, she became hotter with each passing moment. An effusive fire spread through her body all the way to her fingertips and right down to her toes.

When Clay came up for air, he locked the door.

She protested, "We have to stop."

"Why? This is more private than my guest bedroom."

"You're not serious."

"I'm entirely serious. Take a chance for a change, Celeste. Jump off the cliff with me."

Did he think she wasn't capable of adventure? That she couldn't live life to the fullest? He'd thrown the proverbial gauntlet down before her, and she felt destined to pick it up.

Reaching between them, she cupped him. He was hard, fully aroused, and she'd never been so excited in her life. There was something so forbidden about this, so taboo, so secret on so many levels.

While he kissed her again, he lifted her skirt and found only lace panties.

Her name was a guttural groan as he broke away from her to stare into her eyes. Then he was pushing her panties down her legs, dropping his trousers and briefs, leaning into her against the wall.

Restless and excited beyond measure, she ran her nails down his backside. That seemed to be the caress that broke his dam of restraint. He lifted her off the floor until her legs surrounded him. Then he thrust into her, fulfilling every one of her fantasies. Propped against the wall, she ran her hands through his hair, murmuring his name. He pressed into her again and again and again, building the tension, winding it tighter, until suddenly she was filled completely with him, at one with him. The light in the closet seemed to shatter into ten thousand firecrackers, all exploding at the same time. She shook from the impact, feeling weightless in Clay's arms... feeling as if she'd melted into him. Clay's release came as he drove into her one more time and then shuddered with his climax.

Afterward, they didn't move. They just held on, letting the tremors of erotic pleasure subside.

Eventually he murmured against her ear, "If I let your legs drop, can you stand?"

That was a very good question. "I don't know." Her voice was wobbly, and she knew he could hear the tremor.

"Let's try it," he suggested. "Or we both might end up in a heap on the floor."

He loosened his grip enough that she could let her legs fall. He pressed against her, leaning them both against the wall, just in case their limbs wouldn't hold them up.

"Hot sex in a supply closet," he muttered. "Who would have thought?"

That's exactly what this was—sex. By giving in to sheer desire, had she given up something? Had she given up the chance to tell Clay what she really felt? And what about what his father had done? Should she tell him about *that?*

"Is that enough for you?" she asked as an opener, knowing he might stall the conversation completely, especially in here, like this, when they were supposed to be in the Great Hall.

"Are you saying that isn't enough for you?"

He was too practiced at guarding himself, unwilling to show any vulnerability.

When she didn't answer, he asked, "Having regrets already?"

"No regrets," she assured him quickly. She couldn't have regrets when she'd dreamed of this for so long, could she? What was that old saying? Be careful what you wish for because you might get it? The thing was, she'd wished for a lot more. Was Clay capable of committing to a woman again? Or a relationship? Or a marriage?

"I know Zoie hurt you—" she began.

He put his fingers over her lips. "No. No mention of her here. This is about us. I think we need some time together alone."

"What do you suggest?"

"Dad's going out of town on business on Sunday. I can ask Mom if she'd mind watching Abby overnight. I think you and I should ride up to Horsethief Canyon and camp out."

An overnight with Clay in his element and in hers. What could be more romantic or private or intimate? "I like the idea," she agreed.

He gave her one of those crooked smiles and then kissed her forehead. "We'd better get dressed and get back in there."

"Can I ask you a question first?"

"Okay."

"Did this happen tonight because you were jealous?"

After a few moments, he answered, "To be honest, I'm not sure."

Her heart began to fall until he added, "It was the impetus, but it wasn't the cause. Damn it, Celeste, look where we left off Sunday night! Do you believe I didn't think about that when I wasn't distracted by something else? When I close my eyes at night, I can feel you in my arms again. I *wanted* you in my arms again. So tonight? Yes, I was jealous. But what happened in here was going to happen soon somewhere. The tinder caught and I don't believe there's any going back."

He was right about that, but what happened now if he didn't want to delve deeper into a relationship and she did? What happened if they tried to go back?

Maybe on Sunday they'd both find the answers they were looking for.

Clay's hand felt sensual and possessive in the small of Celeste's back as he guided her toward the table where his family was seated. The speaker was finished, and almost everyone was delaying leaving by chitchatting with friends and neighbors.

Clay bent close to her ear. "I'd ask you to come home with me tonight, but I think we'd better keep things low-key for now, don't you?"

Low-key. Exactly what did *that* mean? That he wasn't ready to announce they were seeing each other, sleeping with each other, becoming involved with each other? Still, she'd be with him the day after tomorrow, all alone with no distractions.

"I understand. But I would like to spend some time with Abby tomorrow if that's okay."

"That's fine. She always looks forward to seeing you."

Celeste took a deep breath. She wanted Abby to do more than look forward to seeing her. More each day, she wanted her to consider her as her mother. Yet she knew she couldn't rush anything, even though she desperately longed to.

Harold Sullivan was standing at his place as if he were

ready to leave, though Violet was still seated, speaking with the woman next to her.

As they approached, Violet spotted them. When they were within speaking distance, she said, "Celeste, don't you look beautiful tonight."

"She does," Clay agreed. "Somehow her seating card had the wrong table assignment on it."

"Oh, my! I'm sorry that happened. There were some women I wanted you to meet. In fact, Vanessa Duncan, this is Celeste Wells. She's going to help me with my research for that family history I was telling you about."

Vanessa seemed to be around Violet's age. "It's good to meet you, Celeste. I'm head of the Preservation Committee. If you can spare some time, we can always use your computer abilities. Getting a new museum up and running will be a huge task."

"We can talk about it sometime," Celeste said politely, feeling Harold Sullivan's gaze on her.

After a few minutes of conversation, Vanessa excused herself.

Harold studied Celeste and Clay, looking as intimidating as always. Celeste didn't glance away. She would *not* be intimidated by him. Was he assessing whether or not she'd told Clay about his offer?

Clay had kept his hand on her back, supporting her, supporting them. He said to his mother, "Celeste's going to stop in and spend some time with Abby tomorrow."

"Wonderful. Perhaps you can show me more about Google."

Celeste laughed. "You picked up the basics without any problem."

"Mom, are you free Sunday evening into Monday? I'd like to leave Sunday afternoon for Feather Peak and take Celeste with me. I think we'll camp overnight in Horsethief Canyon."

Clay's dad turned a shade of red. "Do you think that's appropriate?"

"Camping is what I do, Dad, and I've decided to take a friend along to do it."

With a knowing smile, Violet studied the two of them. "It's a great idea. Winter will be moving in shortly, so this could be a last chance to enjoy it."

Harold bent down to his wife and said in a low voice, "How can you condone this?"

Violet shot him a scolding look. "Everyone deserves some happiness. Clay is divorced and Celeste is single. They're two adults who can do whatever they want."

The exchange embarrassed Celeste and possibly Clay, too. He shifted his arm to around her waist and addressed his mother. "You're sure you're okay with babysitting?"

Violet assured him, "When your father's away, I just ramble around alone in that house. Caring for Abby makes me feel worthwhile."

Harold cast a frustrated glance at all of them. "I'm going to the car. I'll wait for you there." He stalked out.

Violet stood then. "I'm sorry if that embarrassed both of you. You know he doesn't like to be thwarted and I've been doing that more and more." She smiled at Clay. "I'm learning lessons from you."

Clay didn't return the smile. "I don't want to make things difficult for you with Dad."

"You're not." Before she turned away, she said, "It's nice to see smiles on your faces for a change." Then she followed her husband outside.

Conflicted, Celeste watched Clay's mom leave. It was

obvious Violet Sullivan knew nothing about the offer her husband had made. As far as Celeste was concerned, she was going to keep it to herself. She wouldn't hurt Clay *or* his mother.

Clay looked over the room and saw Jesse speaking with Noah. "Anyone else you want to talk to before we leave?"

"No," Celeste said with certainty. "I'm ready if you are."

If Clay caught her underlying meaning, he didn't acknowledge it. But he did grin at her. "Once the parking lot thins out, I can give you a decent kiss good-night."

Celeste's heart leapt at the idea of kissing Clay again. Yet the idea that he wanted to keep their relationship under wraps still bothered her.

Would he ever be able to freely admit he had feelings for his ex-wife's sister?

Chapter Eleven

"Clouds are moving in," Clay told Celeste as they passed the trailhead to Moonshadow Mountain and headed for Horsethief Canyon and Feather Peak.

"Do you think they'll cause us trouble?"

"We could get wet," he said, wondering how she'd take that news. This time of year, no one could predict the weather.

"Do you want to turn back?" she asked, slowing her horse.

"Do you?"

She gave him an impish smile. "I won't melt."

He laughed, and it felt so good to do it. Celeste was more of an adventurer than he'd ever thought. He could make a comparison, but he was determined not to. This trip was about the present, not the past *or* the future for that matter.

"How long has it been since you've been riding?"

he asked, noticing she had a great seat and had seemed comfortable on her horse since they'd started out.

"A few years...before Abby was born."

Celeste's life seemed to be divided into before and after her surrogacy. Now there might be another division with her new relationship with her daughter.

She continued, "I've always been grateful that Jenny lets me take a horse out when I visit Miners Bluff. She and Silas both trust me. That's nice to know."

Was there a hidden message there? Was she angling to find out if *he* trusted her?

He realized he did trust her with Abby.

Celeste was wearing a leather hat today, with a horse-hair chin tie and a fleece poncho in a Native American motif. With her boots and jeans and spirited attitude, she was the picture of a cowgirl. Who would have thought?

As they slowed and ambled over rocks and a hillock, she leaned down and seemed to whisper in her horse's ear.

"What's that about?" She'd done it earlier as the miles crept behind them. He was so curious about every facet of her personality now. What was he looking for? Deep-seated selfishness that would affect her ability to nurture Abby?

"This is one of the horses Jenny rescued. She doesn't let many people ride Coronado, but I seem to have a rapport with him. She told me to murmur in his ear every once in a while and he wouldn't get skittish. He's very intuitive, seems to know where I want to go before I do. I hardly have to tug on his reins at all."

"My guess is he's reading your body language, the pressure of your thighs, the weight of your body when you shift, even simple pressure on the reins."

Horsethief Canyon reached before them as the clouds above it gathered into gray swirls.

Celeste motioned toward Feather Peak, which loomed over the canyon. "Yesterday your mom told me that although the Hopis named the peak, your great-grandfather was instrumental in naming Horsethief Canyon."

"It makes you wonder why, doesn't it?" Clay joked.

She tilted her head and caught his gaze. "You're not suggesting he knew a few horse thieves."

He shrugged and grinned. "I don't know. What does your research tell you?" He knew she'd spent Abby's naptime yesterday with his mom on the computer searching for tidbits of history, delving into sites that held land records.

"Your great-grandfather held several deeds, along with the copper mine. He made quite a fortune for his time. But I don't think those are the details your mom was looking for. She wanted more personal information—marriages, children, that type of thing. I told her we should get the word out in the community because there might be artifacts in people's attics that could be useful. I think she and I might go into Flagstaff some afternoon to a museum there. She thinks they might cooperate in finding and verifying museum-quality relics."

"You two seem to be finding common interests." A little surprised about that, he was pleased, too. His mom had never gotten along with Zoie. But maybe that was because Zoie's air of defiance set his mom on edge. Celeste seemed to try to identify commonalities instead of finding differences.

No comparisons, he warned himself again.

"All these years, I thought your mom was cold," Celeste admitted. "But rather than that, she's just reserved."

"Not my dad, though," Clay said, half in jest. But he

noticed Celeste's expression changed and her face seemed to go a little paler.

"You don't like him, do you?"

She took a few moments before she answered. "I don't know, Clay. He tries to intimidate me. I react by standing up to him, but he makes me nervous. I don't think he really cares to get to know me. He just doesn't want me anywhere near you and Abby."

"He's afraid," Clay responded, knowing he probably understood his father better than anyone.

"You're kidding, right?"

"No, I'm not. He's always afraid something will change his world. He hates the idea of change unless he's the one making things move."

She still looked disbelieving.

"He'd be lost without my mother, did you know that?"

"I don't know if I believe that or not."

"Believe it. He's not the ogre he seems sometimes. Not so long ago, I caught him holding hands with Mom while they were watching TV. They've been married thirty-seven years. They married young and sometimes I think he feels responsible that I took that as a model. I didn't wait because I knew *they* hadn't waited. Something like that."

"Did he advise you not to get married?"

"No, just the opposite. He said Zoie and I could grow up together like he and my mom did. But, hey, I don't want to talk about anything related to the past. This trip's just for you and me."

Celeste looked troubled for a moment as if there were something she wanted to tell him, but then she seemed to reconsider. "I like the idea of concentrating on just the two of us."

Was Celeste hiding something? He hoped not. If he found out she was, that could be the end of what was starting between them.

The clouds seemed to hang lower as they trotted over sage, forged into thicker brush, noticed the scenery around them change. The earth became redder, the rocks became tall boulders. Feather Peak loomed up ahead.

A fine mist began falling. "I have plastic ponchos in my saddle bags," he told Celeste.

"I have one, too," she said. "How much farther?"

"About a mile. You'd better put it on."

Stopping, she reached into her fanny pack, pulling out the plastic covering. But as she tried to unfold it, it almost slipped from her fingers.

"Hold on," he said, catching it in the more forceful wind.

Her horse danced sideways, but she murmured to him and he stilled. She let her hat slip to her back, and Clay eased the poncho over her head. In spite of the rain, she was warm to the touch. Her hair was becoming damp, and he let it slide through his fingers as he adjusted the neck of the garment. They were as close as they could be with the horses side by side, and he thought about kissing her. But there would be time for that. He didn't want to rush anything this time.

"Hat on or off?" he asked now, as the mist turned to drops, and he felt them on his face.

"On," she said, letting the poncho hood drop down her back.

He caught a rain droplet that was falling down her cheek. His finger dragging over her skin seemed to make her tremble. Was she that sensitive to his touch? Did she know she could do the same thing to him?

They stared into each other's eyes for a few long moments, then she said, "You're getting wet."

"My gear's waterproof. But even with rain protection, we're going to get wet. We'd better get moving. I don't like the looks of that black cloud."

Just as he said it, the heavens seemed to open, thunder rumbled, lightning flashed and rain poured down.

"The canyon will provide protection?" she called above the storm's noise.

"Some. But make sure you don't take Coronado through the streambed. It can get deep very fast."

"Do you have a place in mind where we can pitch the tents?"

"I think we're going to forgo the tents. There are a couple of caves up there. They'll be better protection against the storm."

"What about the horses?"

This was Celeste, a woman who apparently cared about animals as much as humans. "I'll find an overhang. Don't worry. They'll be fine, too."

"You've been through this before."

"Many times. Trust me."

With his words, she turned his way. He did see trust in her eyes, and that shook him as much as any kiss could. Did he want that trust? Was he ready for it?

Red-brown earth seemed to ooze down the mountain. They wanted to hurry, but they had to be careful because of the horses. The animals could easily slip and injure themselves. Soon, however, they were winding along the canyon trail, thunder and lightning still rumbling and flashing overhead. The walls of the canyon buffered them, although rain still fell between the embankments.

Clay knew, in spite of her plastic outerwear, Celeste

was probably wet. But she wasn't complaining. She was forging ahead with him intent on reaching their destination. Was she pretending, or was this truly part of her character?

He wished he wasn't so cynical. He wished he could believe her optimism was a huge part of who she was. He'd seen it again and again with Abby, so why couldn't he believe in it?

No looking back, at least not for twenty-four hours.

He led the way, picking the trail carefully. Rain dripped down the sides of the canyon, making artistic patterns and free-form shapes between junipers and black walnut trees.

He saw Celeste studying the walls, too. "It's beautiful, isn't it?" she asked.

"Sure is." But he was looking at her.

She must have felt his gaze, because she turned away from the terra-cotta striations and focused solely on him. Her targeted attention gave him a heady feeling of desire that made him yearn to touch her, to be with her. That's what this trip was all about.

Purposefully, he turned toward the sound of the water running in the streambed to distract himself. He wasn't going to jump Celeste's bones as soon as they made camp.

As rain drizzled down, he gestured to the wide trail and the overhangs a story above them. "Let me go first," he said. "Light's dimming and the ground could crumble. I want to make sure it's safe."

"You're the expert," she agreed with a smile, a smile that turned him on all over again.

Wind blew across the top of the canyon. They were mostly protected by the walls, but it brought with it cooler temperatures. Clay took the trail slowly so Celeste would, too. Whenever he camped in the canyon, he usually set up on the floor. But tonight was different.

Patches of ground and rock slid under his horse's hooves now and then. But for the most part, the trail was solid, maybe even well-used. He wondered if teenagers still came up here to make out or if hiking this far was too strenuous an activity these days. Since his father and Silas Decker were friends, he'd always had access to a horse to ride here or wherever he preferred. He was grateful for that.

He brought his horse to a stop when they reached more level ground and waited for Celeste to catch up.

"I'm surprised someone hasn't made a tourist attraction of this place," she said.

"The town fathers won't let anyone do that. The proposal comes up every once in a while but the council always votes it down."

"Thank goodness."

"Tourists still ride up here, but it's far enough away from the beaten track, and it's not well-publicized. Even tourists who make the effort to come here don't want to see it spoiled."

Clay dismounted, tethered his horse to some brush but held hers for her. When she dismounted, he moved in closer, caught her around the waist and eased her to the ground. The rain fell in a light mist again, but they hardly noticed. Her back was still to him, and he folded his arms around her, pulling her against him. There were layers between them—his jacket, her rain gear and poncho. A colder wind whistled across the top of the canyon, slipped inside and bounced around a bit. Still, he held her and she leaned into him.

"We're getting wetter," she whispered.

Waiting a minute for his pulse rate to slow, he unfolded

his arms from around her and backed away. "I know. Let me check out the cave. There are still black bears in the area as well as other critters. I don't want you to meet any of them."

With that, he pulled a knife from his saddlebag and lifted a fallen tree limb from the trail. Then he headed for the black cavern where he hoped they could spend the night.

Celeste shivered as she waited for Clay. This trip was like something from a dream—a fantasy she'd conjured up years ago. Were she and Clay destined to be together? Or was she just a blip on his radar screen, a means to physical satisfaction without really getting involved? If they were going to parent together, they'd have to maintain a relationship for a very long time. How did that play into this chemistry between them?

Clay exited the cave and beckoned to her. "There's a natural chimney in here…so we can light a fire."

There was something that had been on her mind, and she might as well put it to rest. "Can I ask you something?"

"Sure."

"Did you ever bring Zoie up here?"

At first she thought he looked a bit angry that she'd asked, but then he shook his head. "I wouldn't do that to you, Celeste. I wouldn't go over the same path I went with her. Don't you realize that?"

She could just murmur she was sorry, but that wasn't the kind of relationship she wanted with Clay. "Everyone has favorite places, ways they do things, patterns they follow. I wasn't suggesting you'd do anything intentionally. I just had to know."

"Know this," he said, folding his arms around her,

pulling her close. The rims of their hats brushed, and he swiped his off, jamming it into his jacket pocket.

His lips covered hers so seductively she almost fell at his feet. As quickly as he'd started the kiss, he ended it. "I never brought Zoie here. She wouldn't have wanted to get her boots muddy."

With that, he went to his horse and began to unpack their gear.

Celeste helped Clay carry their supplies into the cave, though he told her to stay in the dry. She didn't. She wanted him to see she'd share the burden or the joy of whatever they were doing. The thing was, he still seemed a little miffed at her question, and her lips still tingled from his kiss.

Inside the cave, she realized it was amazingly clean. When she said so, Clay responded, "I think someone recently swept it out. You can see the drag of the branches on the ground." He pointed out the lines and squiggles, and she saw what he meant. There was even a stack of dry wood against one wall.

"That was considerate of them."

"For the most part, campers care where they go and how they leave it. It's a karma thing."

"Karma?"

"Sure. Give good karma. Get good karma back."

When she studied his face, she saw that he meant it. "Is that the way you live your life?" she asked quietly.

"I try to. How about you?"

"It's basically the Golden Rule, wouldn't you say?"

"I suppose." He took the bedroll from its waterproof covering and spread it on the ground. "I'll get some pine boughs to put under this if I can find dry ones. That will be softer."

"Is there anything I can do?"

"How about unpacking the food? Save the granola bars for breakfast. The peanut-butter sandwiches and the chocolate bars and raisins are for dinner tonight and lunch tomorrow."

She glanced toward the stone ring and ashes where other fires had been tended. "I feel as if we've stepped back in time."

"In a way, we have. No cell phones, no TVs, no electricity. I think that's one of the things I like best about guiding."

In spite of the cave's shelter, a shiver slipped up Celeste's back. She'd pulled off the outer plastic covering but her poncho was damp and she had to admit she was getting cold. She wrapped her arms around herself, and Clay noticed.

"One fire coming up. There's not enough wood here to last all night, so we'll have to go easy with it." He made quick work of starting the campfire. It crackled to life in a few minutes.

"I'll be fine," she told him and knew she would be... because she was with him.

Clay made several forays out into the weather, to tend to the horses, to gather the pine boughs, to check other caves for wood. Celeste sat by the fire, staring into it for answers, waiting for Clay to join her. Finally he sat beside her cross-legged, handing her a peanut-butter sandwich while he took another. They ate in silence for a while and sipped water from their bottles.

Should she tell him about his dad's offer, or shouldn't she? Would he think she was trying to make trouble? Would he believe her? And if his father denied it? She had no proof, even though a few of the bank workers had seen her there. His father could always say she had *asked* for money.

Who would Clay believe?

She shivered and didn't know if it was from her damp clothes, from fear of the situation she'd stepped into or from being so close to Clay, yet unable to touch him freely...to tell him how deep her feelings for him ran.

"Are you still cold?" he asked, obviously attuned to her.

"I'm warming up."

"You should take off your clothes and crawl into the sleeping bag. Hopefully they'll dry by the fire."

Take off your clothes and crawl into the sleeping bag. What exactly would that mean for their night together? Would Clay keep his clothes on? Sleep outside the sleeping bag?

She felt as if every decision she made could cost her something. Shivering again, she found her answer. She needed to get dry.

"I think I will. Don't eat all the chocolate," she teased lightly. The last thing she wanted was for Clay to probe and ask her if anything was wrong.

The cave wasn't that large. It was also very quiet. She knew Clay could hear the rustle of clothes as she unbuttoned her blouse and slipped it off, the click of her unfastening the snap of her jeans, the rasp of the zipper as she pulled it down. She didn't know why—delusional modesty maybe—but she kept on her bra and panties. They were sky-blue and lacy and filmy and totally unsuited for a camping trip. But that hadn't mattered. She'd imagined tonight would be special.

She didn't have to worry about Clay watching her because he didn't glance over his shoulder once. It was as if he was totally disinterested.

But maybe he was just as confused as she was. That

idea gave her the courage to ask, "Are you going to watch the fire all night?"

It had already burned down into a low glow. After a pause, he answered, "No. Do you have your flashlight?"

She'd been in such a hurry to scurry into the sleeping bag, she hadn't even thought of it. "No, I don't, but I can—" She reached for her blouse.

"I'll get it for you." He'd brought in the saddle with the saddlebags and heaped everything in the corner farthest from the fire.

Clay had also removed his jacket. His sweatshirt underneath pulled taut across his shoulders and upper arms as he crouched at the saddles and rummaged in her bag for the flashlight. He didn't seem to mind his damp cargo pants. She supposed he was used to this...living out of his saddlebag, dealing with the weather, camping in caves. She could probably get used to it, too, if she could learn some tips from him.

But tips from Clay on survival camping weren't even on her list right now. She was engrossed in the way his hair curled over his collar, by the fit of his pants on his backside, by his sureness and authority in handling himself out here. He was so sexy that just looking at him made her mouth go dry.

Clay found her flashlight as well as his. He brought them over to the double sleeping bag, set his on one side and crossed to where her blouse lay.

"I'll set it here," he said, kneeling down and placing it on top of her clothes.

She needed to know if he wanted her. She needed to know if the other night had been simply an anomaly. Hiking herself up on her elbows, the sleeping bag slipped to her waist.

Clay stared at her, at the blue filmy lace barely covering her breasts, at the thin satin straps, and at her hair falling over her shoulders almost to the clasp.

"Celeste," he breathed as if he couldn't help himself.

She held her breath and waited.

The fire hissed and popped. Wisps of smoke circled to the opening above. She glanced away from him, not knowing what she should do, not wanting her vulnerability to show.

"Look at me," he commanded.

When she did, he came closer and took her chin in his hand.

"I want us both to be sure. I want us both to realize what we're doing. Because I won't be able to stop after one kiss."

His raspy voice and the image he created sent heat flashing through her body. Still she kept silent. She couldn't make another move. She felt as if she'd made them all, and now it was his turn.

"There are nights," he said roughly, "when I camp outside and sleep under that immense sky. I look up and I can't find a single star. But sometimes, if I stay awake long enough, a veil lifts before my eyes and suddenly there are hundreds of tiny lights making the whole trip worthwhile."

In the silence, Celeste could hear the rain rolling off rocks outside the cave. "So the veil has lifted? Do you know what you want?" she asked bravely.

The scent of hardwood burning low wafted around them as Clay answered, "I want *you*."

"I want you, too," she said clearly so he'd know she was as sure as he was.

The intensity in his eyes mesmerized her, and he shifted from his crouch and knelt beside her. Then his hands were in her hair, his mouth was on hers, and she didn't have to wonder anymore whether or not he really wanted her. The other night had been frantic and fast. Tonight—

A wild yearning infused Clay's kisses as a deep fervor provoked the slice of his tongue. She responded in kind, and everything went out of control and hot. His hands went to her breasts and teased her nipples under her bra until she thought she'd come right then and there. She plucked at the V-neck of his shirt, eager for him to be at least as naked as she was. He broke away, only for as long as it took to tug his shirt over his head, unzip his pants and shake off his boots with the rest of his clothes. After he pulled back the sleeping bag, he covered her with his body.

"I want you naked," he growled against her ear.

"Be my guest," she whispered breathlessly, wondering what he would do.

He rolled her with him to their sides, and while he kissed her neck, he unfastened her bra. No sooner had he done that than his lips were on her nipple, and she cried out from the pleasure. His hands seemed to be everywhere, making her mindless, creating urgency that he thwarted by postponing their physical reunion.

"You're not playing fair," she managed to say.

"Tonight isn't about fair. It's about pleasure and passion and getting what we both want."

And just what *was* that, she wondered fleetingly.

He slid lower. As he removed her panties, his mouth and tongue slid to her most intimate places. She knew she wanted a life with him, and she prayed he wanted the same.

But if he doesn't? echoed the faraway thought.

As her body wound tighter, and he brought her to

climax with his mouth, she didn't listen to that faraway question or think about the answer.

She was still tingling from the best orgasm she'd ever had when he rose above her and thrust inside of her.

"Oh, Clay! You feel so wonderful."

"So do you." Moving in and out, he drove harder, finally touching the spot with his finger that had given her so much pleasure minutes before. She cried out so loud, she believed the sound had to echo throughout the whole canyon. As she held on to Clay's shoulders, he found his release with a growl of satisfaction that made her hold him even tighter.

As she held him, and he held her, she knew she'd found bliss. Just how long would it last?

Chapter Twelve

Harold Sullivan let himself into his Chicago hotel room, then let the door bang shut behind him. He flipped over the night lock and crossed the room to the minibar. Opening it, he selected one of the small bottles of bourbon. It was going to be a long night with room service and cable TV, and an even longer day of meetings tomorrow. He missed Violet. He always missed Violet when he was traveling. Their time together lately had been almost contentious, all because of Clay and the choices he made.

Finding an old-fashioned glass the five-star hotel staff had left for him, he filled it with ice from the full bucket and glanced at the bed, which was turned down. He'd paid through the nose for the services.

Heaving himself onto the loveseat in the sitting area, he realized he was in trouble—trouble with Violet and trouble with Clay. Foolishly trying to smooth out his son's life, he'd put himself in a position where Celeste Wells could blackmail him.

He'd been absolutely flabbergasted when she hadn't taken the money, though he had tried not to let it show. Who would have thought? Zoie would have taken that money in an instant.

And that's where he'd made his mistake. What if Celeste really cared about Abby? What if she truly cared about his son? How was he going to be able to go forward with his family after what he'd done?

If he told Violet, in the mood she was in these days, she might leave him. Still, if she found out from someone else, she most definitely *could* leave him, couldn't she? His own wife was changing, and he didn't understand it. She'd been excited about delving into the computer world with Celeste, for goodness sake. How out of character was that? She'd even told him she was bored with her bridge club! She'd belonged to that bridge club for fifteen years. All the wives were married to important men in the community. Cocktail parties with them helped to foster his networking. Yet Violet was thinking about *quitting*.

What had she said to him when he'd left? She couldn't wait to take care of Abby because their granddaughter would keep her young at heart, and she wanted to be young at heart until the day she died. It was about time they both learned how.

He drank half the bourbon in the old-fashioned glass.

Was Celeste the type of woman who would blackmail him? And what would she want, if not money?

It was too dangerous a question to ask...or answer. He'd better fix this somehow himself before his world fell apart.

Celeste awakened in Clay's arms Monday morning. They'd only gotten a few hours of sleep. She couldn't believe the night of pleasure they'd shared, or how that pleasure had excited her as well as terrified her. What if they didn't work out? What if everything fell apart? What if Clay only wanted sex? This morning she had to find out what was going through his mind and what she meant to him.

"It's about time, sleepyhead." His morning voice was sexy and deep.

"Have you been awake long?" She looked up at him, not knowing what she'd see.

"Long enough. Are you cold?"

"Not when you're holding me."

He gave her a grin that made her stomach somersault. "I did more than hold you last night."

She continued to study his face. "What did it mean, Clay?"

This wasn't a conversation he wanted to have—she could tell by the furrow between his brows and the set of his jaw. "I'm still raw from a marriage that didn't work out. And you—aren't you still leery about relationships because of what happened with the pilot?"

It almost sounded as if he wanted her to be. But she'd fallen deeply in love with Clay. She saw now she'd entered into a relationship with Peter because she'd felt it was time to be married and have a family, not because of some great undying love for him.

"But Clay—" Her feelings for him had started developing so very long ago. She'd kept them in check. She'd denied them. With what was building between them, she couldn't deny what was real for her anymore. On the other hand, she didn't think Clay was ready to hear about it.

"I'm ready for a new life," she told him.

"You mean being a mom to Abby."

"I mean, being someone special to *you*, too."

"You are," he said huskily. "But it's not like we can even live together in Miners Bluff. That would kill your reputation, and every town busybody would have a field day. We have to care about that for Abby's sake."

She knew they did. Abby came first and above all else. Yet on the other hand, was she herself always going to be an appendage? Not someone necessary for Clay to live and breathe, as he was to her? She felt hurt that he couldn't say more, couldn't give her more, wasn't willing to do more.

"So I'm going to have visitation days with Abby, and we'll go on from there?"

"*Ample* visitation," he said with a wiggle of his brow. "For me *and* Abby." When he realized how that sounded, he shook his head. "I don't have the answers right now, Celeste."

"You're thinking about what happens if you and I stop seeing each other."

"I have to think about that."

"Maybe. On the other hand, you need to know that when I make a commitment, I keep it." She couldn't make herself any more clear than that except to say she loved him.

Still she saw the doubts in his eyes, the memory of Zoie's affair and her abdication of responsibility. The only course Celeste could take was to love Clay the best she could, to love him until he realized she wasn't going anywhere. Unless, of course, he didn't want her...unless he shut down and pushed her away.

He turned on his side to face her and slid his fingers into her hair. "I have to check on the horses, but before I do..."

His kiss was a continuation of everything they'd shared in the middle of the night. When his hands slid up and down her back and pressed her against him, she had no doubt that he wanted her. But was it a physical need or an emotional one?

They were both breathing hard when he broke the kiss. She thought he might pull away, but he didn't. Instead he asked in a low voice, "How would you like to stay with me and Abby tonight? I'm sure she missed you."

"Is that the only reason?"

"No! I want another night like last night. How about you?"

Yes, she did, but she wanted a future, too. For now, however, she'd take another day with her daughter and with Clay. "I'd love to stay with you tonight."

The next kiss was even longer and wetter and deeper. Lost in it, she almost forgot the question—where did they go from here?

That night, Celeste sat on the side of Abby's bed and pulled the covers up over her. Lulu was tucked under her arm. When Abby looked up at her with such sweet innocent green eyes, Celeste's heart beat madly with the joy she was feeling. "You're going to have lots of wonderful dreams tonight, sweetheart."

Celeste could feel Clay watching from the bookshelf where he was putting the book away that they'd read to her.

Suddenly Abby sat up again and flung her arms around Celeste's neck. "I like it when you're here." The words were a bit sleepy but completely understandable.

"I like being here." She gave Abby a kiss on the cheek and held on tight until her daughter pulled away and slid down under the covers again.

By this time, Clay was at his daughter's bedside, too. He stooped down, gave her a kiss on the forehead and assured her, "Sometime soon I'll take you along to see the mountain, okay?"

"Okay," she agreed with a sleepy smile as she turned on her side and closed her eyes.

Celeste waited for Clay in the hall as he took a last long look at his daughter. They'd made love that morning before they'd watched the sun's first rays stream over the canyon wall. Outside, they'd ridden the horses toward Feather Peak, hiked a bit along its switchbacks and eaten lunch overlooking the valley between Feather Peak and Moonshadow Mountain. They'd kissed often, held hands and laughed in the beautiful sunshine. Celeste had felt so at one with Clay and hoped he felt the same with her.

Abby had been waiting for him with Clay's mom and had excitedly shown them the pictures she'd drawn for them while they were away. They'd spent the rest of the day with her, making her the center of their world.

It had been a perfect day.

And now she and Clay might have another perfect night.

He came up behind her in the hall and wrapped his arms around her. She looked up at him over her shoulder, so sure of what she wanted.

"What now?" she asked with a little coyness to tease him.

"We could find a closet again," he joked as his hand found one of her breasts.

Electric pulses seemed to slash through her body, and the sexual tension between her and Clay was at a fever pitch already.

He turned her to him in his arms. "I'd like nothing

better than to take you to my bed and keep you there all night, but we need to give Abby time to fall asleep."

"I know we do. How about an old-fashioned date?"

He eyed her warily. "And what would that be?"

"Popcorn and a movie. You've got a stack of DVDs in there. I'm sure we can find something we both like."

And it didn't take them long until they did. It was one of those adventure thrillers with just enough action for Clay and just enough romance for Celeste. They microwaved a bag of popcorn, poured it into a bowl, uncapped two beers and settled on the great-room couch. Clay switched on Abby's monitor so they could hear her if she needed them. Then close together, shoulders brushing, they lounged on the sofa, feet propped on the coffee table.

The movie was good, but Celeste was conscious of Clay's every movement. As he glanced at her often, she knew he was conscious of hers. When the popcorn bowl was as empty as their bottles of beer, he paused the DVD, sat against the arm of the sofa and opened his arms to her.

"Come here. There's no reason why we can't be a lot cozier while we wait for her to go into a deep sleep."

Celeste smiled, settled between Clay's legs, her head on his chest, his arms around her. She loved his strength, his sense of responsibility and simply the way he made her feel as a woman.

The movie played once more, and he bent his head to nuzzle her neck. "Your hair drives me crazy," he said in a husky voice. "It slides over your shoulder, swishes across your back, and I just want to run my hands through it."

"Go ahead," she invited, in what was meant to be a playful tone that came out breathless and excited.

His callused fingers slid against her temple, ruffled

her bangs, smoothed over her shoulder. Celeste could feel his arousal. He had the power to turn her on so easily. "I love the feel of your beard stubble against my cheek, your fingers on my skin."

"I want your mouth," he growled, as they shifted so they were lying facing each other, Celeste on the inside of the sofa. Then he took her mouth, and she tried to give him everything she was in the kiss.

"Isn't *this* just *too* cozy?"

Celeste heard her twin's voice and at first thought she was imagining things. Yet as Clay's body went tense, as he raised his head and looked toward the foyer, she knew she wasn't imagining anything.

"She still has a key," Clay muttered as he got to his feet and faced his ex-wife. "What are you doing here, Zoie?"

"I thought I could bunk in your guest bedroom tonight. It was late when I got in, but I can see now this was a terrifically bad idea. Don't worry. I can go to a motel so you can keep doing what you were doing."

Zoie's gaze on Celeste almost made her feel as if she'd betrayed her sister. Had she? Was being here with Clay all wrong?

"How are you?" Celeste asked her sister, afraid to go to her for a hug, afraid she'd be rejected. After all, wasn't she trying to take Zoie's place? Wasn't she trying to become Abby's mother and Clay's permanent lover?

"I don't think I'm quite as fine as *you*. How long has this been going on?"

"That's none of your business," Clay said. "You wanted out free and clear so out you are."

Celeste wasn't sure but she thought she saw sadness— and regret—flicker in Zoie's eyes. As Clay and Zoie stared at each other, suddenly Celeste didn't know exactly where she *did* fit in.

Now also on her feet, she approached Zoie. "I came to Miners Bluff for the reunion," she explained, then amended, "Not just for the reunion. I intended to get to know Abby. She's *my* daughter, too."

For a change, Zoie seemed at a loss for words, as if she'd never expected Celeste to step into the void that she'd created. Then the regret on her face faded, and a defensive wall took its place. She tucked her hands into the pockets of her designer sweater and looked Clay straight in the eye. "You know, don't you, Celeste probably wants to be involved with you simply to become a mother to Abby."

Celeste felt Zoie's words lance her heart. This was her sister, the person she'd been closer to than any other for the first twenty years of their lives. She didn't understand Zoie anymore. How could she be so resentful when she hadn't wanted a life with Clay and Abby, when she'd walked away from everything? But even worse than the loss of that closeness with her twin was the expression on Clay's face and the doubts she suddenly saw in his eyes. He couldn't believe what Zoie had said was true, could he? How *could* he after the day they'd just spent together? After last night? *Oh, my God,* she thought. *He really doesn't trust me. He really doesn't know me. He thinks I would deceive him to get to Abby.*

Celeste felt sick to her stomach, a little dizzy even. She wanted to sink back onto the couch, yet she knew she had to stand tall and proud. She had to stand up for herself in a way she never had before, either to her sister or to Clay.

"As I said..." Zoie took a few steps back. "I'll get a

motel room. As soon as I can arrange it, I'll pick up my settlement and be gone."

Clay's tone was even and controlled when he said, "I could have wired it to you."

"You could have, but I was constantly traveling."

Taking a few steps toward her sister, feeling sorry for her, hurting for her, wishing she knew what she could do for her, Celeste offered, "Abby's sleeping if you want to take a peek."

But Zoie was already shaking her head. "No." She looked at Clay. "I guess we'll have to figure out what we're going to tell her. Or have you already made up a story?"

"I won't make up a story," he said evenly. "I'll tell her some kind of version of the truth that she can understand."

Zoie once again looked from Clay to Celeste and then at the monitor on the side table. "We can talk tomorrow. I should have called before I came. I just never imagined... I didn't realize—"

"What?" Clay asked, when she didn't go on.

"That my coming back could mess up everybody's lives."

"Your leaving did that," he said bitterly, but Zoie didn't even flinch. She just turned around and left again.

The silence that filled the room after the closing of the front door was heavy and stunning. Celeste felt as if she'd been swirled around and turned upside down. And when she looked at Clay, she knew she had to confront those doubts in his eyes.

"That was unexpected," Celeste said, to start somewhere.

"Zoie always does the unexpected. It was fun for a

while, when we had no responsibilities, when we were kids instead of adults."

"I'm not talking about Zoie." Celeste's head was buzzing with her thoughts, confusion and the conclusion she'd arrived at in only a few minutes.

"Excuse me?"

"What did you think, Clay, when Zoie suggested I just want to be involved with you to be a mother to Abby?"

He remained silent.

"*That's* what was unexpected. After last night, after today, I never thought you'd doubt me."

"Wouldn't you if you were in my shoes?"

She tried to look at their situation from his perspective. She really did. But one fact kept her from being able to do that. "I can't put myself in your shoes, Clay, because there's one very big difference between us. I fell in love with you."

The look on his face was total disbelief.

"I see you don't believe that, either. I had a crush on you in high school. I hid it well, though I think Zoie knew about it. You only saw me as a fellow classmate back then, as maybe a friend. You liked girls who were flashier, who had more style. When you started dating Zoie, I knew I didn't have a chance, so I disappeared into the background."

Clay looked as if he were trying to absorb what she was saying but was having a difficult time of it.

"You and Zoie got engaged and married. I found my own life and I thought I was happy. But then Zoie was in that accident and seemed devastated, though I didn't know exactly why at the time. I didn't know about the affair. So when she asked me to become her surrogate, I thought she wanted a family as much as I did. I knew I'd be helping you become a father as well as her become a mother. I knew you'd be a terrific dad."

"How could you possibly know that?" His voice was low...slow, as if he was trying to work through what she was telling him.

"It was easy to see," she responded, remembering. "When brothers or sisters of our friends came around, you were great with them. When our English class mentored third graders and you read to them, I saw how you cared about children. It's one of the reasons I became a surrogate for you. I thought I was giving you a gift. I never imagined giving up Abby would be so difficult. I kept telling myself I had no rights. I had made a promise and I would keep it. Until Zoie sent me that email telling me about the affair, how unhappy she'd been for a long time, that she wasn't living the life she wanted."

Clay shook his head. "I didn't realize how selfish she was. Not until the affair. Maybe even not until after we had Abby and she couldn't seem to bond with her."

"Right. You couldn't see how selfish she was, and you believe I'm the same. You believe I would do anything to get what I want, including sleep with you."

"Celeste." The sound of her name was filled with his frustration and his turmoil.

"I'm *not* Zoie, Clay. I could never pretend something I don't feel. But you think I could. You think I could give my body to you, give my heart to you, in order to become Abby's mother. You don't know me, Clay. You don't know me any more than you really knew Zoie when you married her."

Celeste couldn't stay here with him. She couldn't get her thoughts straight. She couldn't figure out what she should do next while she was in his presence. All she could remember was the doubt in his eyes and his consideration that she could have deceived him. She loved him, but she couldn't convince him of anything. After what Zoie had done, he might never trust a woman again. She couldn't stand to see the questions in his eyes. She couldn't stand the thought that he'd believe that she was with him only because of Abby.

"I'm going back to Mikala's. We'll sort out my time with Abby in a few days."

"You can stay tonight."

She knew he meant in the guest bedroom. "No, I can't. That would hurt too much."

She picked up her purse and duffel bag that she'd dropped just inside the great room when Abby had come running to greet her earlier. How could everything change so drastically in a matter of a few hours?

When she picked up her things and walked toward the door, Clay didn't call her name. He didn't come after her. He didn't stop her. So she left, too, not letting the tears run down her cheeks until she was sitting in her car, backing out of Clay's driveway, heading toward the Purple Pansy.

She loved Clay Sullivan, but he didn't return that love. She'd made a mistake giving him her heart. Now she had to reclaim it and get on with her life.

The temperature had dropped into the forties last night. Still, at seven in the morning Celeste was having coffee with Mikala in the garden at the Purple Pansy when they heard footsteps on the flagstone path around the corner.

"Maybe Clay?" Mikala asked, giving Celeste hope.

"Not heavy enough," she answered, looking down at the phone book where she'd circled the number of the police department. She was going to call Noah to check about his grandmother's vacant apartment.

Mikala and Anna had told her she could stay here as long as she wanted. But Celeste wanted a place of her own where Abby could feel at home. She was really trying not to think of Clay. Every once in a while, she had to blink fast as tears came to her eyes. This time the dream was smashed permanently, and that was a pain that went so deep she couldn't find the bottom of it.

A few moments later their visitor walked around the corner of the bed-and-breakfast, down the purple-and-yellow chrysanthemum-lined path to the small patio.

It was Zoie.

"A little cool for coffee out here, isn't it?" she asked, rubbing her hands.

Not even a greeting, Celeste thought. That was so typical of Zoie. "I needed my mind cleared and numbed," Celeste returned.

Zoie looked surprised at the frank comment coming from her twin, who was usually low-key and caring.

Mikala stood, motioning her to the high-backed rocker she'd just vacated. "It's good to see you again, Zoie. Here, have a seat. I have to help Anna."

"Good to see you, too, Mikala."

Mikala's glance at Celeste was kind and encouraging. Although this wasn't what she'd planned for this morning, Celeste knew she couldn't avoid this confrontation with Zoie. Not for her own sake, but for Abby's. On the other hand, she wanted to feel the bond again that she'd once known with her sister. Maybe there was a way to make that happen.

She assessed Zoie's impeccably tailored pants under her long sweater. "Did you bring any practical clothes along?"

Zoie's brow lifted. "What do you mean by practical?"

"Hiking clothes."

"No, of course not. Why would I need those?"

"Because I want you to climb Moonshadow Mountain with me."

Chapter Thirteen

"Are you going to tell my why you're dragging me up here?" Zoie asked as the sun streamed down on her perfectly styled blond hair.

They had climbed the trail mostly in silence, both of them lost in their thoughts. Celeste hoped that would change once they reached Starfall Point, which wasn't far in front of them now.

"I brought you for the experience."

"I had enough of this when I was a kid and there was nothing else to do."

"I can remember a time when you thought it was fun to climb up here."

That seemed to throw Zoie back into silence until they'd climbed another half hour and reached the look-out.

Zoie didn't hesitate to follow Celeste to the guardrail where they stood side by side, looking down over the valley and Miners Bluff where they'd come to dream of a different life. "What are you trying to do, Celeste? Resurrect old memories?"

"Maybe. Or maybe old feelings. Between *us* anyway."

The wind blew past them, sending loose brush flying.

Celeste turned to Zoie, "Why did you come back?"

"You know why. The rest of the money."

"We're living in the computer age, Zoie. Money can be wired at the click of a key, even to Cannes. Why did you come back?"

Zoie's green eyes were troubled, her expression conflicted.

Celeste waited until finally she warned, "I want the truth."

"I've always told you the truth."

"You didn't tell me about your affair when it happened."

"No," Zoie admitted. "But after the accident, I told you Clay and I were in counseling."

"I thought that was about the hysterectomy and not being able to have kids."

"It was." She put her hands on the guardrail and squeezed tight, looking down on the town. "I was ashamed. Clay knew what I'd done and I had to live with that. I didn't want you looking at me the way he did."

"Clay had every right to be angry and hurt. What did you expect?"

"I didn't think, all right? I met Thad and there was a spark there. Clay and I were growing apart. Marriage wasn't what I expected it to be and I was *trapped*."

"But you did love Clay once, didn't you?"

"Oh, I don't know, sis. I was seventeen when I fell

'in love.'" She made quote marks in the air. "What did I know? Being his girlfriend made me feel secure. You and I *never* had any security. Then when Mom died, I hung on to him. Marriage seemed the perfect solution for the life I wanted."

"You knew Clay loved nature and animals and exploring."

"I thought he'd grow out of it. He was getting a business degree along with his degree in environmental sciences. I thought guiding was a hobby, not what he wanted to do with the rest of his life."

"Didn't you talk about it?"

"We were newlyweds. I don't know. I guess I just never expected him to go against his dad. He graduated, he went to work for his dad and then he decided that wasn't what he wanted to do with the rest of his life. It was like he married me under false pretenses."

"Zoie."

"All right. So maybe he thought he was getting a homemaker and a woman who wanted to be pregnant every two years when he married me. But I figured out that wasn't what I wanted. I didn't meet Thad until four years after we married. And then, I guess, I just wanted to be reckless."

"And after the accident?"

Zoie let out a heavy sigh that fell over the cliff. "I could have been killed. I was driving too fast, going to meet Thad, and I wasn't even sure why. He didn't love me. I didn't really love him. I was rebelling against a life I didn't want. After the accident, Clay said we could try and work out what was wrong with our marriage if we went to counseling. I intended to make it work! I did. I knew what Clay wanted to hear. What the counselor wanted to hear. We had some really close moments. I thought if we had a baby, that would help, too. But after you gave us Abby, I realized I didn't want responsibility for that tiny little life twenty-four hours a day, seven days a week! Not even with Clay's help. That just wasn't *me*."

More than anyone, Celeste understood that Zoie was still trying to find herself. "So why did you come back? Because of Clay? Is there still something there?"

"Gosh, no. That's long over."

"Abby?"

"I haven't seen her for a year. She probably doesn't even remember me." Zoie's voice was wistful and regretful.

"You're her mom."

"So are you. And I think you're probably much better at it than I would ever be."

"What do you want, Zoie?"

"I don't know. I'd like to see her now and then. I'd like to know how she's doing. But I don't want to mess her up. I don't even know if Clay will let me see her."

"Clay will do what's best for Abby."

"You will, too," Zoie said with certainty, because they *did* know each other. They were twins. "Can I be Abby's aunt? Can't we just switch places? That's what you want, isn't it?"

Celeste knew what she wanted. But what she wanted and what she could have were two different things.

"You and Clay seem to fit."

"He doesn't trust me."

"Because of me. But you're not me. He *will* trust you in time. It looked as if you had some pizzazz between you."

Oh, they had pizzazz. Was this a matter of staying and committing herself to Clay and Abby so that eventually he'd realize what she was made of?

Zoie suddenly turned to Celeste and said, "I've made a mess of my life. I know that. But I really don't want to make a mess of Abby's. I think you could be the mom she needs. I might not want to take care of her, but I don't want to lose her, and I don't want to lose you. I'll go to Clay, and I'll tell him I was wrong about what I said. You would never pretend to be into him just to have Abby. I don't know where you got it, but you have integrity."

That was a high compliment coming from Zoie.

"Can you forgive me for what I said to him?" Zoie asked.

Celeste knew Zoie's words had just brought doubts to the surface that Clay had been having all along. They would have had to deal with them at some point. She didn't know if he would deal with them now...if he would ever believe she loved him...as well as Abby.

Thinking about the childhood she and Zoie had shared, the love that used to be so easy between them, the twin bond that tied them together for a lifetime, she said, "Yes, I forgive you."

That night Abby had another bad dream. When she called "Daddy" with tears in her voice, Clay ran into her bedroom, took her in his arms and asked, "What's wrong, ladybug?"

"Where's C'leste? I want C'leste."

He wanted her, too. So many thoughts and conflicted feelings swarmed in his head that he wasn't sure what to think. But he did know one thing. "I'm sure she's thinking about you right now. I'll call her and see if she can come for a visit. Okay?"

Abby nodded and burrowed into his shoulder. He held her until she fell asleep, and then he gently laid her in her bed beside the cat Celeste had brought her and brushed his hand over her forehead, wishing her wonderful dreams.

For the past twenty-four hours he hadn't done much except care for Abby and consider things Celeste had said since she'd been back in Miners Bluff. Things like—*Were you away as much as you were for the business you were building or because you were trying to escape something in your marriage?*

Someday Abby will have to know the truth.

When I make a commitment, I keep it. I fell in love with you.

I fell in love with you.

Clay had gone to the kitchen and was making a pot of coffee—he wasn't going to sleep tonight anyway—when his doorbell rang.

Celeste. Could it be Celeste?

No. He'd done irreparable damage there. She wouldn't be knocking at his door anytime soon. Not unless it was for Abby's sake.

When he found out who his visitor was, he couldn't believe his eyes. "Dad!"

His father looked as uncomfortable as he'd ever seen him. He was still wearing his suit with his tie tugged down. "I had a meeting and I wanted to wait until Abby was asleep. Is she?"

What could bring his father to his door this time of night? He *never* came just to chat. He never came just to see Abby. So what was this all about?

"She had a bad dream and I just put her back to sleep again."

"Can we talk?"

His father wanted to *talk*. Clay tried to absorb that. "Is this about my retirement account?"

"Hardly. This is important, son."

When had his father last called him "son?" He stood aside, inviting his dad in.

They settled in the great room, his father in the recliner, Clay on the sofa. "Is something wrong with Mom?"

"Other than the fact that she's thinking about leaving me?"

"What?"

"If I can make this right, I think she'll forgive me. Women are better at forgiving than men, don't you think?"

"I haven't really thought about it."

"Well, we can hope, because from what I've heard, you've got some ground to cover, too."

"What have you heard?" Clay asked warily.

"Apparently your mother called Celeste about getting together to look at her family history documents. You know your mother. She asked about the camping trip, et cetera. Celeste told her the two of you had had words and she didn't know when she'd be seeing you, though she was hoping you'd let her see Abby."

"I wouldn't keep her from Abby." Clay rubbed his hand over his face. Just thinking about all of it made his heart sink, made his stomach turn. "So what does this have to do with you and Mom?"

"I offered Celeste money."

That couldn't mean what Clay thought it meant. Before he rushed to some absurd conclusion, he'd better hear his dad out. He waited.

"I don't mean that trust fund for Abby or anything like that." Now his dad stood and paced across the room. He seemed to have trouble looking Clay in the eye, and that's when Clay knew they were in for a bumpy ride.

"You'd better finish explaining before I jump to the wrong conclusion."

"Your conclusion would probably be right." His father's gaze finally met his as he stood still. "I offered Celeste half a million dollars to go away and leave you and Abby alone."

Clay jumped to his feet, anger rushing into every particle of his body. But before he could get a word out, his dad held up his hand to stop him. "She wouldn't take it. She said money had nothing to do with why she was here."

Clay's fury must have shown clearly in his eyes because his father started shaking his head. "I know I've interfered before. I know I shouldn't have interfered now. But I just couldn't bear the thought of a woman taking you across again. You have blinders on when you get involved. Just look at what Zoie did to you. I was only trying to help."

Clay took several deep breaths to calm down. "Are you apologizing or defending yourself? Because if this is the way you told Mom, no wonder she wanted to walk out."

His father seemed to grow smaller in front of his eyes. His shoulders slumped a little, and his back wasn't quite as straight. "I know. I don't really think she meant she'd leave me. She was just so mad. She went up to the bedroom and slammed the door."

For his father to say all this to Clay—Clay knew he indeed had to be upset. But there was only one thing he cared about. "When did you offer Celeste the money?"

"The day of the fundraiser. I asked her to come to the bank and she did. She didn't even have to think about it. She tore up the check, threw it on my desk and left. And listening to your mom and thinking about how Celeste has cared for Abby...I finally can believe she cares about you and Abby."

His father believed that, yet Clay had doubted her. What did *that* say? "Zoie's back," he informed his father without inflection.

His father's brows raised. "No one told me *that*."

"She still has a key to the house and she came in while Celeste and I were...kissing."

The nerve in his dad's jaw twitched, but he didn't say anything. He just waited as Clay had.

"Zoie was surprised, flustered, I guess a bit angry. She made the comment that Celeste was just involved with me so she could have access to Abby. I...considered it."

Silence pulled between them until his father broke it. "You doubted Celeste's motives, too."

"I know she wants to be a mother to Abby. And we'd had a wonderful overnight trip that I could hardly believe. But in that moment, when Zoie made the remark, I thought about her pretending to be happy, pretending to want a family, pretending we still had something when we didn't, and I couldn't help but wonder if Celeste was pretending, too."

His father crossed to the sofa and sank down onto it. Clay did the same.

"How do you feel about her now?" his dad asked.

"I feel as if I've cut a bond I need as much as air to breathe. I feel as if I've destroyed what we've built. It's only been twenty-four hours and I miss her and what she brings to my life."

"So, what do we do?" His father's voice was filled with the same remorse and regret Clay was experiencing.

"So I think we'd both better hope that we're in love with women who have kind hearts and know how to forgive," Clay answered.

His father asked, "Do you have any beer?"

Clay went to get two.

Celeste didn't know why Mikala had suggested she go to the music store with her and then out to dinner. She supposed her friend was just trying to cheer her up. That was tough. Tomorrow she'd have to call Clay to see about Abby. She wasn't going to let too many days go by without visiting her, but her heart hurt when she thought about it…whenever she thought about Clay.

When she slipped the old-fashioned key into her door after saying good-night to Mikala, she was surprised when she found it unlocked. She was sure she had locked it before she left. But then she'd been absentminded the past few days, so maybe she *had* forgotten.

As soon as she walked into the suite, she knew she hadn't forgotten, and someone had been here. There was a huge, round lit candle on the coffee table, smaller candles on the sofa side tables and the desk. Rose petals were strewn in a path around the coffee table.

Clay stepped into her line of sight. There was a serious expression on his face and emotion in his eyes. "I hope you like it," he said, his voice gruff as if this wasn't easy for him.

"I'm not sure what it means," she replied honestly, her pulse racing, her heart thumping so hard she thought it would pound through her chest.

He came toward her then and held out his hand. "Sit with me."

She was glad he suggested it because her knees were shaking. They sat beside each other on the sofa, their shoulders brushing but their bodies tense because neither of them knew what to expect.

"I owe you an apology," he began.

"Clay—"

"Let me finish this or I'll forget things I want to say."

She almost smiled at that but didn't because those things could push her out of his life.

"I should have known better than to think your motives were anything but pure. And I'll tell you why. I remember the girl you were in high school, and I know the woman you are now. The past two months with me and Abby, you've been genuine, no pretense, no guile because you don't have that in you. I knew that but I still let Zoie's words affect me. I'm sorry for that."

His apology was so unexpected she didn't know what to say.

So he continued, "Dad came over to visit last night."

Now she almost felt as if she'd faint. What had his dad said about her? Had he lied and said she *did* take the check? Did he want her out of his son's life that much?

She managed to pull her voice from somewhere down her throat. "What did your father want to talk about?"

"He wanted to confess what he'd done. Apparently he told my mother last night and she wasn't too happy about it, either. He told me he offered you money to leave Miners Bluff...so you'd walk away from Abby and me."

She was so shocked. When she realized her mouth was open, she closed it. "He actually told you that?"

"He did. He was shaken up about it, too. Apparently my mother was so mad she threatened to leave. He didn't want to lose her, and he didn't want to lose me. That was a surprise. I always thought I was a thorn in his side."

She was glad Clay's father had finally told him how he felt. "I wanted to tell you about his offer, but I was afraid it would hurt you."

Clay took her hand between the two of his. "You were

afraid if you told me, there would be an even bigger wedge between me and my dad. I got that right away. But his telling me that, it just reinforced how wrong I was to even consider what Zoie said."

He shifted on the sofa cushion and brought her hand to his lips. She began to cry even before he said with so much sincerity she couldn't doubt him, "Celeste, I love you. I never wanted to fall in love again. I don't think I even wanted to consider a serious relationship again. But then I danced with you at the reunion and something about you got to me. It was more than attraction. It was your determination to be a mother to Abby. You didn't just feel it was a duty or responsibility. You *wanted* to be a mother. At first I thought, oh, that's great in theory. After a few days of it, you'd give up. After a few visits, you'd get tired of it. But that didn't happen. And when Abby was sick, you took care of her so kindly, compassionately, so lovingly, I knew what you were telling me was true. You wanted to be a mother and you were going to be one whether I wanted you to be or not. It had nothing to do with the bond that was growing between us. It had everything to do with your relationship with Abby."

When he paused, she had to jump in. "Did you say you love me?"

"Oh, yes, Celeste. I love you with all my heart. And—"

He rose, then bent down on one knee in front of her on the rose petals he'd so carefully strewn about.

She was crying seriously now. Tears ran down her cheek into the corner of her mouth.

Clay smiled and gently wiped them away. Pulling a black velvet box from his pocket, he opened it.

She saw a beautiful diamond in an antique setting secured in the velvet. "Oh, Clay."

"I hope that means you like it. Celeste Wells, will you be my wife?"

In a flash of comprehensive awareness, she realized he was proposing! "Yes, of course I will. Oh, Clay, I love you so much. I've been so afraid you'd never trust me. But I was just going to stay here and show you and Abby how much I love you no matter how long it took."

Clasping her hand, he slipped the ring on her finger. "I want you to stay here for a lifetime. I want you to stay with me for a lifetime. I'm going to look for a business partner and cut back my trips."

"No. You love doing what you do."

"I love you more. And," he said with a wink, "you and I will be taking some of those trips together, down to the bottom of the Grand Canyon, rafting on the Colorado River, hiking up Moonshadow Mountain. We'll go alone and we'll take Abby, too. We'll have a wonderful life, Celeste, if we both work at it. We both know marriage is give-and-take. But mostly giving because we love Abby and maybe, just maybe, we can give her a brother or sister some day."

At that, Celeste threw her arms around Clay's neck and hugged him hard. He rose with her to his feet, holding her close.

When he kissed her, Celeste knew he was promising her a lifetime of adventure and love because that's who Clay Sullivan was—a man who knew the importance of a promise.

Epilogue

Early October

Celeste put the finishing touches on Abby's hair by tying a rose ribbon around a few of her daughter's long ringlets. "There," she said. "All done. And you look so pretty."

Abby's rose-colored dress, which in a few minutes would be covered by a matching coat, suited her perfectly. She would be the perfect flower girl at the perfect wedding.

Abby looked up at Celeste in awe and exclaimed, "*You* look like a pwin-cess."

Celeste laughed, feeling like one. Her satin gown with long sleeves, sweetheart neck, slim waist and tiered layers might make her look like a princess, but Clay made her *feel* like one. In spite of orders from her bridesmaids not to get wrinkled or mussed, Celeste hugged Abby close, grateful for every minute she had with her, grateful she was going to be her mother.

There was a light rap on the open door to Abby's room. Celeste looked up and saw Zoie.

"Ready for the walk on the runner?" she asked, a smile in her eyes as well as on her lips.

Celeste knew her twin was truly happy for her. In the weeks since they'd trekked up Moonshadow Mountain, Celeste had learned that Zoie was a buyer for a shoe designer—a European shoe designer. He not only appreciated her sense of style, but he'd invited her to spend a few weeks on his yacht when she returned. She'd found a life for herself, even if it wasn't the one Celeste would have chosen. Celeste just hoped the life or her shoe designer would make her happy.

"Aunt Zoie," Abby said. "I'm gonna throw flowers."

Zoie stepped into the room and crouched down before Abby. "Do you know what kind of flowers?"

"No. But they're pink."

Zoie laughed.

Celeste had watched her sister visit with Abby since she'd returned, and Celeste guessed as Abby grew older, she and Zoie could become friends. She and Clay had had a long talk about it, and this seemed to be the best idea. Celeste would step into the role of Abby's mother, and Zoie would be her favorite aunt. There would be plenty of time for explanations and the truth.

Jenny and Mikala now came to the door, too, and beckoned to them. "Come on, the music started. Your mother-in-law-to-be has a wonderful taste in harpists," Mikala noted with a smile.

"And the arbor she helped you select is gorgeous, too," Jenny added. "In fact everything is absolutely beautiful.

Maybe you and Mrs. Sullivan should go into business together planning weddings."

Each day, Celeste was getting to know Violet Sullivan better. She and Harold had even come to terms. He'd visited her just as he had Clay, and he'd apologized. It had seemed sincere. Just last night at the rehearsal dinner, Violet had nudged her husband into making a toast. He'd done it and done it well.

Celeste took Abby's tiny hand in hers. "Let's go get married."

Clay and Celeste had insisted on keeping the wedding small. They'd asked friends and classmates, Mikala's aunt and Silas Decker. Clay's groomsmen, Riley O'Rourke and Noah Stone, escorted guests to their seats.

The time had come for the procession. With a last hug and kiss from Celeste, Abby started down the aisle with her basket, tossing flowers onto the white runner, looking ahead and waving at her dad.

Celeste saw the smiles and heard some chuckles. She liked the way the wedding was getting off the ground. When Mikala and Jenny and then Zoie preceded her, Harold stepped beside her and offered her his arm.

"Thank you for accepting my offer to do this. This was one thing Violet didn't suggest. *I* did."

Celeste studied Harold's face. "I never had a father."

He was obviously taken aback by her comment, and his face flushed a little. "Well, if that's an invitation, I'd like to try to be a stand-in. If I promise not to give too many orders, it might work."

Celeste squeezed his arm and smiled. "It might."

They started down the aisle, and Celeste felt that she and Harold could come to an understanding that could make both of their lives richer.

Before the arbor where the minister and Clay stood,

Harold placed Celeste's hand in Clay's. Dressed in a Western-cut tuxedo, he'd never looked more handsome.

He leaned close to her ear, murmuring, "You take my breath away."

She hoped she could do that for the rest of their lives.

Facing the minister and Moonshadow Mountain, their wedding began.

As the minister opened his book of ceremonies, Clay leaned into her again. "When we go to Horsethief Canyon next weekend, you and I will have our own private ceremony and exchange vows again, okay?"

"More than okay."

Clay's smile, his arm suddenly encircling her waist, told her they would renew their vows often, to remind each other of their promises and commitment. She liked that idea. She liked that her husband-to-be had thought of it. She loved Clay and knew she would until the end of time. She was a happy woman, and she could see from Clay's face, he was a happy man.

The minister began, "Dearly beloved, we are all gathered here—"

Their life together had begun.

* * * * *

Look for the next
REUNION BRIDES *book,*
coming soon to Silhouette Special Edition.

COMING NEXT MONTH

Available February 22, 2011

SPECIAL EDITION

REQUEST YOUR FREE BOOKS!

2 FREE NOVELS PLUS 2 FREE GIFTS!

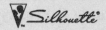

SPECIAL EDITION

Life, Love and Family!

YES! Please send me 2 FREE Silhouette Special Edition® novels and my 2 FREE gifts (gifts are worth about $10). After receiving them, if I don't wish to receive any more books, I can return the shipping statement marked "cancel." If I don't cancel, I will receive 6 brand-new novels every month and be billed just $4.24 per book in the U.S. or $4.99 per book in Canada. That's a saving of at least 15% off the cover price! It's quite a bargain! Shipping and handling is just 50¢ per book in the U.S. and 75¢ per book in Canada.* I understand that accepting the 2 free books and gifts places me under no obligation to buy anything. I can always return a shipment and cancel at any time. Even if I never buy another book, the two free books and gifts are mine to keep forever.

235/335 SDN FC7H

Name	(PLEASE PRINT)
Address	Apt. #
City	State/Prov.	Zip/Postal Code

Signature (if under 18, a parent or guardian must sign)

Mail to the **Reader Service:**
IN U.S.A.: P.O. Box 1867, Buffalo, NY 14240-1867
IN CANADA: P.O. Box 609, Fort Erie, Ontario L2A 5X3

Not valid for current subscribers to Silhouette Special Edition books.

Want to try two free books from another line?
Call 1-800-873-8635 or visit www.ReaderService.com.

* Terms and prices subject to change without notice. Prices do not include applicable taxes. Sales tax applicable in N.Y. Canadian residents will be charged applicable taxes. Offer not valid in Quebec. This offer is limited to one order per household. All orders subject to credit approval. Credit or debit balances in a customer's account(s) may be offset by any other outstanding balance owed by or to the customer. Please allow 4 to 6 weeks for delivery. Offer available while quantities last.

Your Privacy—The Reader Service is committed to protecting your privacy. Our Privacy Policy is available online at www.ReaderService.com or upon request from the Reader Service.

We make a portion of our mailing list available to reputable third parties that offer products we believe may interest you. If you prefer that we not exchange your name with third parties, or if you wish to clarify or modify your communication preferences, please visit us at www.ReaderService.com/consumerschoice or write to us at Reader Service Preference Service, P.O. Box 9062, Buffalo, NY 14269. Include your complete name and address.

USA TODAY *bestselling author Lynne Graham*
is back with a thrilling new trilogy
SECRETLY PREGNANT, CONVENIENTLY WED

Three heroines must marry alpha males to keep
their dreams…but Alejandro, Angelo and Cesario
are not about to be tamed!

Book 1—JEMIMA'S SECRET
Available March 2011 from Harlequin Presents®.

JEMIMA yanked open a drawer in the sideboard to find Alfie's birth certificate. Her son was her husband's child. It was a question of telling the truth whether she liked it or not. She extended the certificate to Alejandro.

"This has to be nonsense," Alejandro asserted.

"Well, if you can find some other way of explaining how I managed to give birth by that date and Alfie not be yours, I'd like to hear it," Jemima challenged.

Alejandro glanced up, golden eyes bright as blades and as dangerous. "All this proves is that you must still have been pregnant when you walked out on our marriage. It does not automatically follow that the child is mine."

"'I know it doesn't suit you to hear this news now and I really didn't want to tell you. But I can't lie to you about it. Someday Alfie may want to look you up and get acquainted."

"If what you have just told me is the truth, if that little boy does prove to be mine, it was vindictive and extremely selfish of you to leave me in ignorance!"

Jemima paled. "When I left you, I had no idea that I was still pregnant."

"Two years is a long period of time, yet you made no attempt to inform me that I might be a father. I will want DNA tests to confirm your claim before I make any decision about what I want to do."

"Do as you like," she told him curtly. "*I* know who Alfie's father is and there has never been any doubt of his identity."

"I will make arrangements for the tests to be carried out and I will see you again when the result is available," Alejandro drawled with lashings of dark Spanish masculine reserve.

"I'll contact a solicitor and start the divorce," Jemima proffered in turn.

Alejandro's eyes narrowed in a piercing scrutiny that made her uncomfortable. "It would be foolish to do anything before we have that DNA result."

"I disagree," Jemima flashed back. "I should have applied for a divorce the minute I left you!"

Alejandro quirked an ebony brow. "And why didn't you?"

Jemima dealt him a fulminating glance but said nothing, merely moving past him to open her front door in a blunt invitation for him to leave.

"I'll be in touch," he delivered on the doorstep.

What is Alejandro's next move? Perhaps rekindling their marriage is the only solution! But will Jemima agree?

Find out in Lynne Graham's
exciting new romance
JEMIMA'S SECRET

Available March 2011
from Harlequin Presents®.

HPEXP0311

Start your Best Body today with these top 3 nutrition tips!

1. **SHOP THE PERIMETER OF THE GROCERY STORE:** The good stuff—fruits, veggies, lean proteins and dairy—always line the outer edges of the store. When you veer into the center aisles, you enter the temptation zone, where the unhealthy foods live.

2. **WATCH PORTION SIZES:** Most portion sizes in restaurants are nearly twice the size of a true serving and at home, it's easy to "clean your plate." Use these easy serving guidelines:
   - Protein: the palm of your hand
   - Grains or Fruit: a cup of your hand
   - Veggies: the palm of two open hands

3. **USE THE RAINBOW RULE FOR PRODUCE:** Your produce drawers should be filled with every color of fruits and vegetables. The greater the variety, the more vitamins and other nutrients you add to your diet.

Find these and many more helpful tips in

YOUR BEST BODY NOW
by
TOSCA RENO
WITH STACY BAKER

Bestselling Author of
THE EAT-CLEAN DIET®

Available wherever books are sold!

NTRSERIESFEB

Silhouette *Desire*

USA TODAY bestselling author

ELIZABETH BEVARLY

is back with a steamy and powerful story.

Gavin Mason is furious and vows revenge on high-price, high-society girl Violet Tandy. Her novel is said to be fiction, but everyone *knows* she's referring to Gavin as a client in her memoir. The tension builds when they learn not to judge a book by its cover.

THE BILLIONAIRE GETS HIS WAY

Available February wherever books are sold.

Always Powerful, Passionate and Provocative.

Visit Silhouette Books at www.eHarlequin.com

SD73078